What Happened on

FOX Street

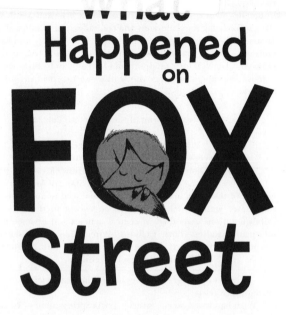

Tricia Springstubb

BALZER + BRAY
An Imprint of HarperCollins*Publishers*

For invaluable insights and unwavering belief in this story and
in me, my deep appreciation goes to Donna Bray and Sarah G.
Davies. For being my champions and comrades, the incomparable
Tahoe Girls—Mary Grimm, Susan Grimm, Mary Norris, and Kris
Ohlson—deserve many thanks. An overdue thank-you to the
Ohio Arts Council for its support. But for Paul, after thirty-seven
years of love and sustenance, no words—he can read my mind
and heart.

Library of Congress Cataloging-in-Publication Data
Springstubb, Tricia.
    What happened on Fox Street / Tricia Springstubb. — 1st ed.
        p. cm.
    Summary: Fox Street means everything to Mo Wren, who is
nearly eleven, and so she is very upset when a land developer offers
to buy her father's house, especially since she has not yet found the
fox she is sure lives in the nearby ravine.
    ISBN 978-0-06-198635-2 (trade bdg. : alk. paper)
    [1. Neighborhoods—Fiction.   2. Real estate development—
Fiction.   3. Fathers and daughters—Fiction.   4. Best friends—
Fiction.   5. Friendship—Fiction.   6. Family life—Ohio—Fiction.
7. Ohio—Fiction.]   I. Title.
PZ7.S76847Wgm   2010   2009053563
[Fic]—dc22   CIP
                                                          AC

Typography by Sarah Hoy
10 11 12 13 14   LP/RRDB   10 9 8 7 6 5 4 3 2 1
❖
First Edition

For Kelly, our family's newest reader

The Thinker, Part 1

FOX STREET WAS A DEAD END. In Mo Wren's opinion, this was only one of many wonderful, distinguishing things about it.

It was a short street, five houses on either side, smooshed close together but in a nice way, like friendly people in a crowded elevator. A piano player lived here, and a teacher, not to mention a man who fixed things, a woman who worked in a funeral home, and the two best burrito makers in the city. If you thought about it—and Mo did a lot of thinking—just about your every need could be satisfied on Fox Street.

There was even a mean, spooky old lady, if ringing

doorbells then running away, or leaving dead mice in mailboxes, was your idea of fun.

Paradise Avenue bordered one end, and the ravine the other. Mo Wren's house was in the middle, where a heart would be, had Fox Street been a person. Sparrows nested under the eaves. This summer a crop of maple trees had sprouted in the gutters. Nature loved that little house as much as Mo did.

She personally had drawn every breath of her life here, having been born a week early and in a great headlong rush, in the very kitchen where she now stood, ten years later, on a boiling June day, fixing her father's lunch. Mr. Wren had a softball game this afternoon, which meant he was in an excellent mood, for a change. He sat reading the sports pages, his dark, curly hair peeking out from under his cap. Mo's father was handsome as a movie star, everyone on Fox Street agreed.

"Want chips, Daddy?"

"You're a mind reader."

"I knew you were going to say that."

Fist bumps! She set his sandwich in front of him and sat down. The wooden table was inscribed with dark hieroglyphicish slashes and crescents. Mo's mother had been an absentminded person, prone to forgetting things like setting a hot pad beneath a skillet or casserole dish. She'd always played music while she cooked, and when Mr. Wren came home they'd kiss for a while, then dance. Back then Mo's feet could fit right on top of her father's, and they'd all whirl around till a pot started boiling over.

"You're not eating?" Mr. Wren asked.

Mo shifted in her chair, unsticking her thighs. It was fiery hot in the little kitchen, hotter even than outside, where the Cleveland cicadas buzzed like rattlesnakes that had learned to climb trees.

"Mercedes is coming," Mo reminded her father. "I'll be eating at Da's."

Mr. Wren pushed back his cap. "Mercedes! My third-favorite kid in the world."

Mercedes Walcott was Mo's best friend. She lived down south in Cincinnati but spent every summer across the street with her grandmother. Mo counted the days till her friend arrived. Deeply as Mo loved Fox Street, she was forced to admit it lacked two things:

1. Foxes.
2. Girls.

Three things, if you counted her mother. But Mo tried not to do that.

"This calls for a toast!" Mr. Wren pulled two cans of pop from the refrigerator just as the phone rang. He swore under his breath. "That better not be work."

But it was.

"You gotta be kidding me, Jake! Not again! Public Square?" He yanked off his cap and threw it on the table. "Man, I feel the pain. But no way can I come in. I got serious car trouble. Not to mention a . . . a root canal appointment in half an hour. And—what?"

He broke off, scowling. With one finger, Mo carefully traced a scorched squiggle.

"You trying to say something's wrong with my record?"

Mo traced the squiggle faster. Mr. Wren had been out of work a long time before he landed this job at the water department.

"Yeah yeah yeah, I get it," he said at last. "I'll be there soon as I can get away."

He hung up and mashed his cap back onto his head.

"Forty-two-inch main just blew—that's the second bleepin' time this year. Public Square's a river. Nobody within a mile's got any pressure." He took a swig of pop. "It's all hands on deck."

4

"Wow. You better get your uniform on, Daddy."

He set the can down and clasped his hands around an invisible bat. The only uniform Mr. Wren had ever wanted to wear was a shortstop's for a major league team. *Slice*—he took a hard cut at an invisible curveball. His runner-up dream was owning his own sports bar. It would be a nice neighborhood place, where families could enjoy a great burger together, and teams could hoist a few after their games. Sometimes he and Mo sat around dreaming up names for it. Home Plate. Time Out. Triple S (for ShortStop Spot). The only thing standing between him and it was scraping together enough for the down payment.

"You and the other guys will be heroes," Mo told him.

"Mud-covered rats, you mean?" He drained the pop. "Mojo, work is the world's most necessary evil."

He tossed the can in the garbage, then pulled a handful of scratched-off lottery tickets from his pocket and threw them away, too. "Sorry. This means you've got to watch Decimal Point the rest of the day."

"I don't mind."

He crooked a finger under her chin. Two lines arched up between his eyes and disappeared into his forehead, forming a tree with no leaves. Mo hated how those lines had dug in deeper every time she looked.

"You're my dependabillibuddy." His arms went around her. Nothing bad could ever happen with those strong arms circling you. "We open the Home Team, you're my manager. Deal?"

He started for the stairs.

"But Daddy?"

He turned around.

"That can't really be true, can it?" she asked. "I mean, 'necessary' and 'evil' can't ever go together, can they?"

When he smiled, his eyes were dark stars.

"What'd I tell you about thinking too much? You're going to get yourself in big trouble one of these days."

Mo retrieved her father's can from the trash and put it in the recycling. She knotted the top of the trash bag, put her untouched pop back in the fridge, then offered the last crumbs of her father's sandwich to two big ants foraging on the kitchen floor.

He was always telling her she thought too much. Which made Mo uneasy for three reasons:

1. She couldn't help it.
2. She thought he could be wrong, not only about this but other things, too.
3. Maybe reason number two proved he was right.

Starchbutt

YOU CAME TO THE END of Fox Street and *kaboom*, the world fell away. The pavement gave out and all you saw was a guardrail and the tops of trees. The guardrail was dented from drivers turning the wrong way out of the Tip Top Club, up on Paradise Avenue, and only realizing their mistake at the next-to-last minute, when they slammed on their brakes just in time to keep from sailing out over the edge and down into the ravine below.

When Mo stepped out of her house, the summer air was tangy and sweet, a mix of city smells from up on Paradise and country perfume from down in that

Green Kingdom. Mo lugged the garbage bag back to the garage. The Wrens shared a driveway with Mrs. Steinbott, and Mo could hear the neighbor's radio, tuned to a talk show whose every caller shouted and sputtered in fury over one thing or another. Starch-butt stayed tuned to that station twenty-four seven.

Every Saturday she boiled her sponges and hung them out to dry on her little line. In today's heat the sponges had already grown stiff as boards. Taur Baggott, one of the way-too-numerous Baggott boys, claimed he'd once watched Mrs. Steinbott trap a cat digging in her rosebushes, and the poor thing was never seen again. Boiled, most likely. Her basement was probably piled with bleached bones.

Mo closed the trash-can lid tight. The animals who populated the ravine considered Fox Street their own personal all-you-can-eat buffet. Raccoons raided trash cans, skunks raised their babies underneath porches, and once Mo had watched a red-tailed hawk swoop down and pluck a pigeon right off the sidewalk in front of the Baggotts' house. Another time a bunch of Tip Top regulars had piled out on the street, shouting and pointing, claiming they'd seen a wild turkey big as a washing machine go by. Not that you could trust those guys.

The only animal no one had ever seen was a fox. Mr. Wren said the chances of spying a fox on Fox Street were about as good as that of spying a band of angels playing harps up on Paradise. And then he laughed. Not his real laugh, but a laugh like something hard hitting something even harder.

She wiped her hands on the grass, which was littered with pale, hard plums no bigger than jelly beans. The plum tree was the best thing about the Wrens' tiny backyard. It had planted itself, some ambitious plum pit recognizing a beautiful spot and making itself at home. Over the years Mo had done her most productive thinking with her back nestled against its trunk. But it was a bad sign for it to be dropping fruit like that— the weather had been so hot and dry, the poor tree was struggling. Mo made a mental note to pull the hose back here and give it a long drink, and then she headed for the street.

Whenever their father was at work, Mo was in charge of her little sister, Dottie, who was half Mo's age but possessed approximately one hundredth of her sense. That wasn't all Dottie's fault, Mo knew. She hadn't had the advantage of their mother very long, for one thing, and Fox Street had ruined her, for another. Everyone watched out for her, not to mention

9

spoiled her rotten, so that at any given moment Dottie could be in Mrs. Petrone's kitchen eating homemade pizza, or on Da's porch being read to, or—this was all too likely—getting into deep doo-doo with the Baggotts.

Then again, she could be up on Paradise or down in the ravine, both forbidden, hunting bottles for her collection. Which she must have done already today, because there on the front walk was a careful arrangement of tall and short, fat and thin bottles. Dottie grouped her bottles into families—mothers, fathers, children, babies. She had aunt and uncle bottles, grandparent bottles, and teenage bottles with names like Tiffany and Rihanna. Hands on hips, Mo scanned the street. The front yards were small enough that you could lean right over your porch railing and have a conversation with your neighbor on the sidewalk, and there was Mr. Hernandez, owner of the restaurant Tortilla Feliz, chatting with Ms. Hugg, the piano player. Mrs. Baggott slouched on her porch swing, pulling on her cigarette, while beside her, Baby Baggott pulled on his bottle. Mr. Wren, wearing his water department uniform, backed the car out of the driveway, tooted the horn, expertly skirted the colossal pothole known as the Crater, and drove out of sight.

But no sign of Dottie.

Just as Mo was about to start hunting for her, Mrs. Steinbott's front door opened and out she came, toting her knitting basket. Starchbutt's hair was fuzzy and white as dandelion fluff, and she herself was skinny as a stalk. At first glance she looked several thousand years old, but look again and you'd see her hands were smooth and her step quick. Mrs. Steinbott whiled away her hours pruning shrubs within an inch of their lives and knitting, though who all those itchy hats and scarves could be for remained a mystery. No one ever came to visit her. Her life was solitary as the unplanet Pluto.

Why was she so alone? And so stone hearted? Which came first? It was as hard to determine as the chicken and the egg, a problem Mo had given some thought to.

"Hello," called Mo.

Starchbutt cocked her head, like a robin just before it nails a poor, unsuspecting worm.

"Your roses are looking good." Mo gestured toward the bushes that bloomed in profusion all around the porch. Their perfect, bugless leaves shone in the sun.

Mrs. Steinbott froze midknit. For a moment, Mo

actually believed she might say, "Why thank you, neighbor." But instead, a furious electric shock seemed to go through her. What in the world could make her shudder like that? Starchbutt raised a shining needle and pointed it across the street.

Mo looked, just in time to see a rubber band of a body sproing out Da's front door.

Mercedes

"Mo!"

"Merce!"

Dodging between the parked cars, Mo tore across the street. Mercedes flung long golden arms around her.

"Merce! You look so different!"

"Mo! You look precisely the same!"

"No I don't!" Mo always talked too loudly around Mercedes Walcott—she couldn't help it. "I grew a whole inch."

Mercedes had always been taller, but this year she'd grown so much that Mo had to step back to look her in the eye. Her laugh was the same, though—head back, gap teeth flashing white against her gingersnap-colored skin. Everything about Mercedes Walcott crackled and bit. The only soft thing about her was her hair. Speaking of her hair . . .

"Merce! You're bald!"

"Really?" Mercedes widened her eyes and ran a hand over the top of her head. "Crudsicles!" Mercedes laughed again. She adored teasing Mo. And Mo didn't mind. Much.

"You shaved it? How come? And how come you're here so early?"

"I took a plane." Mercedes yawned. "Then a cab." She plucked at her jeans, which were black and, Mo suddenly noticed, the precise kind the popular girls at her school wore. Her tank top was black, too, with little sparkles around the edge. Mo smoothed her own baggy, wrinkled shorts.

"Wow," she said. "Cool."

Every June before this—and there had been five so far—Mercedes had ridden the Greyhound out of Cincinnati. Da would send the money for the ticket, and Merce would jump down the bus steps holding one practically empty suitcase. Every August she staggered back up, that suitcase weighted with all the

14

books Da gave her. Da also tried to plump up her only grandchild, but that never took.

"My new stepfather," Mercedes said now, as if those two words carried as much meaning as a whole chapter book. Her mother, who'd never had a husband, had gotten married that winter.

"He's rich?" Mo asked.

"We're *comfortable*," Mercedes replied. "He's got avalanches of money, but don't ever say 'rich.' That's ghetto. You say 'comfortable.'"

"Oh."

Mercedes had a way of raising her chin that elongated her entire self, as if she were about to turn into a human steeple.

"Not that he corrects me," she said. "I have to admit, he's too smart for that."

"Oh." Mo smoothed her wrinkled shorts again. "Soooo, you don't like him?"

"Did I say that? If only it was that simple."

Mo was saved from saying "Oh" again by a voice that had set hundreds of schoolchildren quaking like wind chimes in a high wind.

"Mo Wren!"

Mo told herself that Da didn't try to make her name sound like "moron" on purpose. All the same, she was grateful that Da had retired and there was zero chance of ever having the woman for a teacher. Da was tall as a man. Her beautiful skin had a midnight sheen that reminded Mo of silk or satin, the sort of delicious fabric you long to lay your cheek against.

Her voice, however, was the kind of wool that rubs your neck raw.

"I wasted time, now time doth waste me!" cried Da, who, if she ever went on a quiz show and got Shakespeare for her category, would become an instant millionaire. "Your beans and rice are getting cold, Mo Wren!"

Da's red beans. Mo would choose them for her last meal on Earth. She was already up the front steps before she noticed Mercedes still rooted to the sidewalk. Her best friend stared across the street, past the parked cars gleaming in the sun and Mrs. Steinbott's roses blooming like a piece of heaven, directly at the porch of the tiny, blue-white old lady, who stared steadily back. For a brief, bizarre moment, Mo saw something identical in the way they cocked their heads, as if listening to a bit of music just out of range of everyone else's hearing.

"Mercey!" Mo called, breaking the spell. Her best friend whirled around and ran to join her.

Stumps

BACK WHEN DA STILL TAUGHT SCHOOL, she'd stalked her classroom in shoes adorned with buckles and buttons and rhinestone bows. Da didn't just have smarts—she had style, which made it especially disturbing to watch her clomp down her front hall now in shoes heavy and ugly as miniature coffins.

Stumps. That's what was inside those special shoes. This past winter, Da's sugar had acted up again, and she'd gone into the hospital, missing her daughter's wedding at the last minute. Not only that. When she came out, she left behind four toes.

Clump da clump da clump. Da's shoes and cane beat a

slow rhythm. Mo swallowed hard. Not that she was the squeamish sort. How could she be, living with Dottie, who regularly ate boogers and scabs? The sight of a run-over squirrel? The stink of Baby Baggott's poopy Pampers? Business as usual.

But something about a three-toed foot made her knees wobble. Mo liked things whole. She refused to begin a jigsaw puzzle unless she knew all the pieces were there. A puzzle was nothing compared to your own body.

Da had the table set with her good dishes, yet something wasn't quite right. Normally this house was all about neat corners and polished surfaces, but today it had a dull, unwashed look. Mercedes ran a finger through the dust furring the windowsill and frowned.

But the food! Da's cooking was like an excellent mystery story, with spicy clues and sweet clues and then a great whammy of an ending when it all came together. Mo had just put her napkin in her lap—Da was a stickler for manners and posture—and picked up her fork when the glasses began to shiver and the dishes to tremble. A redheaded torpedo fired into the room, scoring a direct hit on Mercedes.

"You're here!" The Wild Child squashed her face in the vicinity of Mercedes's belly button. "I thought you'd never get here!"

Mercedes managed to peel Mo's little sister off her, all except for a sour-apple lollipop, which hung suspended from her black tank top. Dottie retrieved it and graciously offered it to Da.

"Oh, wait, you can't eat candy. You're diabolic."

"Diabetic!" corrected Mo.

Wrinkling her nose, Mercedes peered down at Dottie's knotty red mane. "Eeyoo! What's that? A fly that got caught and buzzed itself to death?" Mercedes did not exactly return Dottie's affection. In fact, Mercedes preferred not to associate with anyone under four feet tall.

Dottie scrambled up into a chair and lovingly spread Mercedes's napkin across her own lap. She wore an enormous T-shirt advertising hot sauce and, given how much she hated underwear, probably nothing else.

"Your head's like a bowling ball," she said pleasantly. "Dude, it's hot in here. It's hotter than h—"

"Lord give me strength!" Da's face was arguing with itself, her mouth frowning while her eyes danced. "When was the last time those hands met soap and water? No one sits at my table with hands like that!"

She hauled Dottie into the kitchen. Mercedes and

Mo took the opportunity to clean their plates and slip out the front door.

The heart-shaped leaves of a big ancient lilac drenched Da's front porch in shade. If you sat here for a while, Da would pop out with lemonade, or a Band-Aid for the splinter you always got from a floorboard. Those rough, gaping floorboards had a ferocious appetite—over the years Mo had played here, they'd swallowed down more Barbie shoes and game pieces than she could count.

Her mother used to sit here with Da, listening to ball games on the radio. Mo could remember that. Mr. Wren watched on TV, but Da and Mrs. Wren claimed the more you had to imagine, the more exciting a thing was.

"Mo?"

"Yeah?"

"I just had a funny thought. You know all the toys we lost down the porch? Not to mention all the candy wrappers and Popsicle sticks we pushed through the cracks." Mercedes sounded wistful, which was disturbing, since she was not the wistful type. "Imagine someday an archaeologist excavates down there. What would he or she think?'

"That it was the royal burial ground of an ancient

civilization where Uno cards were sacred."

"Where they worshipped tiny plastic shoes." Mercedes laughed, and Mo forgot to be disturbed.

"Not to mention peach pits and repulsive Band-Aids."

Oh, it was good to have Mercedes back!

"Come on," said Mo. "I've got the Den all stocked, and we seriously need to catch up."

Fox Den

THEY SPED PAST MS. HUGG's pink house and then the Petrones', where a hearse took up the whole driveway. Mrs. P styled hair at a funeral parlor, and when she worked late they let her drive the hearse home instead of taking the bus. The Baggott boys—named for signs of the zodiac because Mrs. Baggott believed they'd one day be stars, ha ha—were giving one another rides in a shopping cart stolen from the E-Z Dollar. Pi Baggott, a year older than Mercedes and Mo, practiced skateboard tricks on the edge of the Crater.

"Hey!" he called, flipping his board upright. It was strange. Up until this summer, Mo had never bothered to distinguish one Baggott from another. But all of a sudden, Pi stood out. Pi was impossible to ignore. "Welcome back!" he told Mercedes.

"I can't believe the city didn't fix that pothole yet!" she replied. "It's seriously bigger than last year!"

"Hello to you, too," Pi said.

The daisies were in full bloom, and the butter-and-eggs, too. Mo climbed over the guardrail, careful to avoid the thistles. On the other side, a path meandered down the hillside. Scraggly as they were, the trees clinging to the slope didn't mind if you grabbed their trunks to keep from slipping. As you descended, rocks jutted out like the snouts of buried dinosaurs. And everywhere you looked, the landscape was decorated with trash.

People—no one on Fox Street, Mo was certain, but other people, who were lazy and ignorant—had the notion the ravine was a free dump and heaved all sorts of things over the guardrail, right past the sign that read $100 FINE FOR LITTERING. Mo spotted a wheel-less bike, a broken high chair, a torn lamp-shade. Ghostly garbage bags fluttered in the trees.

Ghostly, but in a good way—this was the feeling Mo always got here. Climbing down the hill, she took her time, making as little noise as she could, her eyes peeled. Fox Street had gotten its name for a reason, and sometimes, especially toward dusk, the air took on a mysterious, deep red texture. At those moments, Mo felt a beautiful pair of amber-colored eyes watching her. She'd sense a rust-colored tail, tip dipped in cream, disappearing just behind her. But no matter how quickly she turned, Mo never saw anything.

Still. Never once did she come down here without being on fox lookout. Light and quick and shy as they were—Mo had read a good deal about foxes—they always saw you before you saw them.

Mo didn't keep secrets. She disliked them nearly as much as she did surprises, which is to say a great deal. And yet, deep inside her, wrapped up as carefully as a fragile glass egg, she cherished, if not exactly a secret, a belief. One she had never confided to anyone. Not even Mercedes.

"Maureen Jewel Wren! Come on!"

Mo believed foxes lived down here. And that they knew she was looking for them.

Or, at least, one fox knew. A certain one, graceful and beautiful, that she had seen in her dreams. And though it might take a very long time, if Mo was patient enough, and persistent and faithful enough, someday that fox was going to reveal herself. To Mo.

"MO!"

"I'm coming!"

Mercedes had already twirled the combination lock on the toolbox and set out cans of Tahitian Treat and bags of chips on the flat rock they used for a table. The Den was a hollow in the side of the hill, not quite big enough to stand up in, shaded and half hidden by an outcrop of rock. Mercedes and Mo had decorated it with things thrown over the guardrail, including the two only slightly ripped beanbag chairs on which they sat.

At the bottom of the ravine, across the stream, stretched the vast city Metropark. Mo could hear the distant cheers of a softball game—the one Mr. Wren was supposed to be playing.

"I can't tell you," Mercedes said, handing Mo a can, "how much I've been looking forward to this very moment."

They clinked cans. Down at the invisible baseball game, a cheer went up.

"Especially since," Mercedes went on, "this is my last summer coming."

Tahitian Treat shot out Mo's nose. "Whaaaaa?"

"It's a miracle I got up here at all. My stepfather registered me for one of those enrichment camps where you learn calculus in the morning and French in the afternoon and for extra big fun you take a trip to a museum. He says a girl with my potential shouldn't waste a whole summer doing nothing."

Mo wiped her sticky chin with a leaf. "Nothing! Is he mental?"

Mercedes nodded.

"It's useless trying to explain to him about Fox Street. He's all about getting ahead in the world. He grew up poor, but he worked hard and took advantage of every opportunity and became an attorney and blah blah blah."

Mercedes paused. She gazed at a spot somewhere over Mo's shoulder. "It's . . . it's weird, Mo. But I'm afraid he's infecting me."

From down on the ball field came a huge, collective moan.

"Infecting?"

Mercedes knotted her fingers. "With the snob virus. Monette and I, we always lived in such butt-ugly apartments. The last one, if you sat on the toilet you had to put your feet in the tub. After you checked for roaches. But now we live in his stupid minimansion, and I . . . I don't know." Mercedes kept her eyes on that spot just beyond Mo. "You get used to nice things. Real fast."

Mo hugged her knees. She searched for the right words.

"But Fox Street is nice."

Mercedes pursed her lips. For no reason, a little rock broke loose from the hillside and tumbled down past them.

"When I got here last night, everything looked so, I don't know. Used up. I told myself it'd look better in the morning, but . . ." Mercedes swallowed. "It looks even worse."

One day last winter, Mo had been hurrying down Fox Street when she'd hit a patch of ice and whomped over flat on her back. All the breath went out of her. Her lungs refused to work, and for an endless moment, Mo lay staring up at the gray metal sky, abandoned by her own body. By the whole universe. This is how lonesome dying feels, she'd thought in terror, just before a great pain stabbed her chest and delicious, frigid air flooded all through her.

That was how it felt now. A shock, and then an outburst.

"Looks!" she said. "You said 'looks.' But *looks* don't matter. It's what's underneath that counts!"

"This gets worse," warned Mercedes.

"How could it? You're disrespecting Fox Street! That means you're disrespecting me, not to mention Da! And speaking of Da, I guess your stepfather—by the way, doesn't this bonehead even have a name? I guess Mr. X doesn't care if he breaks Da's heart, because that's what'll happen if you quit spending summers here."

Mercedes ran her fingertips over her gleaming head. "You didn't even ask me why I shaved my head."

"I did so. You ignored me."

"I did it to make him furious. He's always telling me I look just like my mom, and in his eyes, that's the biggest compliment in the universe."

Mercedes jumped up and started pacing on the edge of the Den, sending up dust clouds.

"He makes her so happy! It drives me bonkers! And now she can afford to quit her dumb job and go to college, the way she always dreamed." Mercedes paced back and forth so fast Mo began to get dizzy, then came to a sudden stop. "It's extremely challenging," she said quietly, "to keep hating him."

Mercedes had never known her father. When Monette had discovered she was pregnant, she'd moved away from Fox Street and never looked back. She refused to even say who he was—he was sweet and he was gone, that was all the information Mercedes had. Here was yet one more way Merce and Mo were alike, beside having identical initials, and being born the very same autumn, and both adoring Fox Street: They were both half orphans.

"He wants me to call him Dad. Ha! They'll fix the Crater before I call him that."

"What *is* his name?" Mo asked.

"Cornelius!" Mercedes cried. "Cornelius Christian Cunningham!"

They looked at each other and burst out laughing.

"Three-C!"

"Lord give me strength!" piped a voice, and Dottie butt skidded down beside them. A licorice whip drooped from her mouth like an extra tongue. Her hair not only was brushed, it had a ribbon in it, making her look like a stray someone had attempted to dress up for a dog show.

"You're more persistent than the plague." Mercedes wiped her eyes. All the merriment drained out of her.

"You all right, Mercey?"

"Do I look like I'm all right?" Mercedes sank back down on her beanbag. When Dottie nestled close, Mercedes didn't even shove her off.

What would it be like never to know one of your

parents? Dottie claimed she had memories of their mother, but she'd only been three when it happened, practically not even human yet, and she also claimed she could read the minds of cats, and fly when no one was looking. She wanted to remember, Mo knew. Could you need something you'd never had, the way you did food, longing for it even before you'd had your first taste? And which was better—having no memories, or memories that made your heart swell with sadness? And—

"That was just the appetizer bad news." Mercedes's voice broke in on her thoughts. "Here's the main-course disaster."

It was quiet now. The ball game must have ended. To calm herself, Mo tried to imagine baby foxes curled up pointy nose to bushy tail in their den.

"I told them I was coming up here this summer if I had to walk the whole way, and they said they understood. I know Monette does. He was probably lying. But they both made me promise one thing before I left."

"What?" Dottie whispered. "What did you promise?"

"To talk Da into selling her house and moving to Cincinnati."

Traitor, Part 1

"BUT YOU KEPT YOUR FINGERS CROSSED, right?" Mo demanded.

"Of course! What kind of traitor do you think I am?"

"So it doesn't count!"

Mercedes threw her hands over her eyes as if she couldn't bear looking at Mo a second longer. "You insist on searching for a bright side, no matter what."

Mo shrank back like a poked pill bug. "Something wrong with that?"

"You don't get it!" Exasperation zapped Mercedes's voice. "Sometimes there *is* no bright side. Okay? Da's getting old! Understand? She's only got six toes."

"But . . . but she gets around fine on those . . ." "Stumps" stuck in Mo's throat.

"Sugar's a treacherous disease," Mercedes lectured. "You can lose your leg if you're not careful."

A bad taste rose in the back of Mo's mouth. A taste that, if it had a color, would be greenish black.

"Monette says Da shouldn't be on her own anymore. Her pension's not big, and she's got too much to worry about between her health and taking care of the house." Mercedes waved her hands in the air. "Not that I agree, but my bedroom? Monster water stains down the walls. It even kind of . . . smells. You know how Da is about cleanliness! That leak in her roof must have gotten bigger. If it rains . . ."

"It's not going to," the Wild Child said soothingly. "Daddy says it's a freaking trout."

"Drought!"

Mercedes sank her poor head into her hands. "It feels like everything's falling apart here."

"Feels!" Mo was on her feet. "Another measly word, just like 'looks'! Nothing to do with the real, actual truth!"

"Go ahead," said Mercedes from behind her hands. "Philosophize away. Be my guest."

"Let me think."

Mo concentrated. She fed a chip crumb to a passing ant, who immediately began dragging it home to share. *Share.* A meteor shower lit up her mind.

"Your mom can move up here!" Mo cried. "Three-C's got oodles of money—let him fix up Da's house. He's a lawyer—he can get a job here easy. And your mom can go to Cleveland State, and we'll all live here together. You and I will be in the same class at school!" Shooting stars, *zing, zing!* "Just like we always wished, Merce! Sleepovers every weekend! You and me, twenty-four seven! It's been nice to know you, Greyhound bus!"

Dottie bent her knees and pretended to stir a big pot. "The dance of victory!" she proclaimed.

But Mercedes shook her head. "Don't you think I already tried that?"

The stars began to fade.

"Monette will never come back. She said good-bye to Fox Street because she'd made a mistake—namely, getting pregnant with me."

"That doesn't make any sense," Mo protested. "Nobody thinks you're a mistake. Not anymore."

Mercedes smiled. "Thanks, Mo."

"It's true! Why does Monette have to be like that? It's too dumb!"

"When she lived here, everybody was so proud of her. After they got over their witless shock at a black family moving onto the street, everybody acknowledged she was brilliant, and stellar, and so excellent at so many things—"

"Like you."

Mercedes smiled again. Mo knew all the stories about Monette—how people predicted she'd go to Harvard, or Hollywood, or who knows.

"Everyone pinned their hopes on her," Mercedes went on. "Well, maybe not Starchbutt. As if she counts." Mercedes bit her lip. "I'd run out of fingers and toes if I tried to count the number of times circumstances have gotten really, really low and I said, 'You know, Monette, we could always move back in with Da.' She always tells me, 'No, we can't. Retreating to Fox Street would be a giant step backward.'"

"I can walk backward. Want to see?" Dottie demonstrated.

Heavyhearted, Mo closed the toolbox and snapped shut the combination lock. They trudged back up the hill. On Fox Street, Ms. Hugg, the piano teacher, perched on her pink steps, painting her toenails the same purple as the streak in her hair. The younger Baggott boys were tearing around the A.O.L. (Absolutely Off Limits) House, machine gunning one another with sticks. As the girls approached, Pi Baggott executed a perfect 180 across the Crater.

"That was for your benefit, Mo," said Mercedes, striding on. "That boy is stupefied with love."

Mo tripped over her own feet.

"Shows what you know, Mercedes Walcott."

"Unless he's stupefied, period."

"All he loves is his skateboard!"

"A blind man could see it."

Mo snuck a glance over her shoulder. Pi stood on the edge of the pothole, and when their eyes met, his lips curved. Those lips! They were the one soft thing in that long skinny face. It was as if Pi Baggott had another, gentler side he couldn't manage to keep secret.

Not that Mo liked secrets.

Up on Mrs. Petrone's porch, the hair trimmer hummed like a bee in your worst nightmare. Mrs. P was giving her boy Nickie his summer buzz cut and waved as they went by.

"Welcome home, Mercedes! Nice hairstyle!"

By now Mercedes's long legs had carried her far ahead of Mo, and she wasn't slowing down. Mo fixed her eyes on her friend's arrow-straight spine. Mercedes was no traitor—she was caught between a rock and a hard place, that was all. Mo dug her fists into the pockets of her shorts. There could be absolutely, positively, without a shadow of a doubt, no question where Mercedes's loyalty lay.

Fox Street without Da and Mercedes? The only thing harder to imagine was Fox Street without the Wrens.

Heartbeat

THE WATER MAIN BREAK turned out to be a lolla-palooza. Mr. Wren still wasn't home by ten that night, so Mo had to let her sister climb in bed with her, which was the only way she'd ever go to sleep. After her bath Dot smelled truly, purely sweet, not her usual artificial-flavoring sweet. Mo had the window open, and that sweetness mingled with the fragrance of Mrs. Steinbott's roses, perfuming the room.

But Mo did not sleep well. She dreamed of a family of foxes in grave danger. Something large and formless stalked them—no sooner did they settle down in their cozy den than they had to flee for their lives, threading between the dark trees, hunting for a safer place. The mother fox stayed far ahead, running so fast the kits kept losing sight of her and the father—where was he? He'd disappeared, *poof!* The small foxes huddled, unsure which way to go.

Her pounding heart woke her. Her sister lay with her arms flung up over her head as if she'd been dropped from the sky. Outside it was middle-of-the-night quiet. Mo ran down the hall.

Her father's bed was empty.

She ran down the stairs, stepping on the beer bottle Dottie had left on the bottom step so someone could break their neck. Mo landed on all fours, her heart in her mouth. She stumbled into the living room.

There he was. On the couch, sound asleep, still wearing his water department uniform. A streak of mud shot across his forehead like a comet.

Mo cupped a hand over her sprinting heart. *Home.* He'd always come home. Always be there. He'd promised her, a hundred times. A thousand times.

Gently, she tugged off his work boots. How heavy they were, soles and laces caked with yellow clay. Mr. Wren stirred, then began to snore with a little *putt-putt* noise, like a boat on a calm sea. Mo went back to bed, and this time she fell sound asleep.

Sundays were quiet on Fox Street. Mercedes had to spend most of the day at church with Da, who couldn't wait to show her off. When Mr. Wren finally got up, he was very grumpy, but Mo talked him into cooking them what he called a restaurant breakfast—eggs, home fries, bacon, a stack of toast drenched in butter. When he owned his own place, breakfast would be on the menu all day long. Afterward he and Mo went out into the backyard to throw the ball around. But the yard was small, and the plum tree got in the way, and though she wanted to keep his spirits up, Mo found playing catch boring. She wasn't sorry when he said he thought he'd join a pickup game over by the middle school, and that Mo and Dottie should meet him at the Tortilla Feliz, up on Paradise, later. They'd get a table out back and order their favorite, the Burro Burrito.

So Mo unkinked the green hose and gave the plum tree a hearty drink. A shiny-winged blackbird, high in its branches, eyed her with approval. Then Mo settled on the front steps while Dottie crouched in the dirt beneath the bushes and held a funeral for a housefly. Mo watched Mrs. Baggott push Baby Baggott in the stroller and wondered how it could be that Mrs. Baggott's flip-flops only went *flop*, not *flip*. Mr. Duong mended a bicycle on his front lawn. The summer sun ricocheted off the roofs of the parked cars and winked in the diamond-paned windows of Da's yellow house. Mrs. Steinbott was clipping the grass around her roses. *Snipsnipsnip,* rhythmic as a heart's beat.

This was the spot where Mo's mother would sit, waiting for Mo to come home from school. As soon as she turned the corner and passed the Kowalskis' hedge, she'd spy her mother's wild, rusty red hair and start to run. In those days, her backpack held maybe one piece of paper and her crayons. It was empty and light. A little kid's burden.

The Kowalskis had moved away a long time ago. The people who lived there now worked the night shift somewhere and slept all day, and nobody ever saw them. Their front windows still said MERRY XMAS in spray-on snow.

"I now pronounce you dead," said Dottie, smoothing the dirt and sprinkling it with dandelions. "Rest in peas, almonds."

Mo flattened her hands on the warm wooden step. The sun was sliding down the sky. A ray slanted onto Mrs. Steinbott's clippers and made them gleam.

Clipclipclip. Everything's going to be okay, Mo told herself. Things will all work out.

Still, she wished she didn't feel so alone. What she needed was a sign. Something real, with a weight she could feel in her hand. Something to anchor her the way, when you did a headstand or a cartwheel, you found a spot on the wall to focus your eyes, so you could keep up, up and down, down.

The Letter, Part 1

THE VERY NEXT DAY, the Wrens received the Letter. Bernard, the mailman, a handsome older man with dreads, delivered it. It was the kind of official mail requiring a signature, and he let Mo sign, since Mr. Wren was at work.

No sooner had she read it than like a pebble from a slingshot, she was across the street and up on Da's porch, where Mercedes sat fanning herself.

"Read this!" Mo commanded.

Mercedes laid down the paper fan, which advertised Mrs. Petrone's funeral parlor. O GRAVE, WHERE IS THY VICTORY? it asked.

"Let me take a moment to introduce myself," Mercedes read aloud. "My name is Robert J. Buckman, and it is my understanding that your property on Fox Street may be available for purchase . . . midst the current economic turmoil, when real estate is so difficult to sell . . ." Mercedes was a speed reader. Her eyes flew down the page faster than her mouth could keep up. "Prepared to make a generous offer . . ."

"I don't get it."

". . . in a position to buy your property in as-is condition . . ." Mercedes narrowed her eyes. ". . . can close the sale quickly . . . am prepared to pay one hundred percent cash . . ."

"I don't get it."

"Unfortunately, I do." Mercedes tossed the letter aside. "One time, a landlord sold our place right out from under us. Monette and I were out on the street"—she snapped her fingers—"just like that."

The normally cool porch grew hotter by the second. Mo's mouth was Sahara dry.

"I don't get it," she rasped, as if saying the same thing three times might break the evil spell.

"A neighborhood goes downhill, and some sleazoid sees his chance to make money." Mercedes started fanning herself like someone single-handedly trying

43

to extinguish a forest fire. "He buys up houses for next to nothing, throws a little paint on them, then resells them for a profit."

"But . . . but why would he send it to my dad? Of all people?"

Mercedes stopped her fanning. She studied Mo. "You might want to ask *him* that question."

Mo did not care for the tone of her best friend's voice. She snatched the letter back and reread it. Phrases like "generous offer" and "one hundred per-cent cash" leaped out like neon signs.

"If my father saw this, that scum-bucket Buckman would be history!" She crumpled the letter in her fist.

Just then Da shuffled out onto the porch, leaning on her cane, a three-pronged contraption that looked designed to support a light or a fan, not a human being. Mercedes hustled to put a pillow behind her and drag over a stool for her feet. When Da plopped down with a small grunt, Mo worked hard not to pic-ture what was inside those shoes.

"Mo Wren! There is no music in the nightingale. Why do you look so upset?"

"I'm not!" Mo shot Mercedes a look that said, No need to worry Da, right?

"We feared a lethal gas attack," Mercedes replied,

cool as can be. "But it was only dear sweet Mrs. Steinbott."

Three heads swiveled to look across the street, where Mrs. Steinbott was spraying her roses from a yellow canister that was nearly as big as she was.

"Those poor bugs." Da gave her head a small shake. "They don't stand a chance."

"Me either," Mercedes said. "Every time I pass her house, I feel her watching me. It creeps me out. I feel like she's counting the hairs on my head. I mean, if there were any hairs."

"Don't be silly." But Da, who'd always taught them how rude it was to stare, in turn regarded Mrs. Steinbott for a long time.

"When Mr. Walcott and I first moved here," she said at last, "Gertrude and I used to sweep our sidewalks every evening. Now, being the first people of color, we Walcotts weren't particularly welcomed. That, my children, is what you call an understatement."

Under normal circumstances, there was nothing Mo loved better than sitting on this porch listening to Da's tales about the old days on Fox Street. Da was big on history. "If you don't know where you're going," she liked to lecture, "you'd best know where you're coming from." Not that Mo planned on going anywhere. Da's Fox Street tales were her tales, too. Sitting on this cool, creaky porch, she loved slipping back to the time when Fox Street was paved with bricks, and the neighborhood was so young, someone else lived in the Wren house. The thought of that made her brain cartwheel.

Now a completely new and previously unthought thought gripped Mo. A thought that was terrible and yet so obvious, so undeniable, it yanked her upright in her chair.

If someone had lived in the Wren house before them, someone else could live there after them.

"Gertrude and I would be out there wielding our brooms, and she wouldn't so much as look at me. Mr. Walcott and I were going to be the ruination of the neighborhood, after all! A month went by, and then another, and by then Mr. Walcott and his green thumb had transformed this front yard into the neighborhood Garden of Eden." She raised her eyes to heaven. "Forgive me, James, for the sorry condition it's in now." Taking the fan from Mercedes, she waved it slowly, wafting memories around.

"By then, all the other neighbors were dropping by to borrow a rake, or investigate that good smell coming from my kitchen, or ask how in the world had I

46

taught Monette to read when she was only three. But not Gertrude. Tidy as she was, with all her life arranged in nice, orderly columns, it seems she couldn't figure out where to classify us Walcotts. So there the two of us were, night after night, keeping to our own sides of Fox Street, for all the world as if we lived on the banks of a crocodile-infested river. Well. One night, didn't she up and nod. And the next, go so far as to call out good evening. Finally Gertrude actually crossed Fox Street to inform me boiling water poured in the sidewalk cracks would kill the ants. It was the first and last complete sentence I ever heard the woman speak."

Da rearranged her toe coffins. Her look grew faintly puzzled, as if a student had written her a good essay but left off the last lines.

"Neither one of us is the warm fuzzy kind," Da said. "There was never a chance we'd be best friends."

Across the street, Mrs. Steinbott thumped her big yellow canister down on the porch.

"I'll never forget the night I went upstairs and found that devil Monette luxuriating in a rose-petal bath, like a princess in one of those fairy tales she loved. The perfume about knocked me over!

She'd snipped off an armload of Gertrude's American Beautys and carried them home. I chased her, naked as a jaybird, all around the house." Da's fan paddled the air. "When she told me Gertrude's son, Walter, egged her on and told her to take as many flowers as she wanted, I had to scold her all over again. I knew Gertrude didn't like those two playing together."

All at once, she'd commanded Mo's attention.

"Mrs. Steinbott had a son?"

Da raised her eyebrows. "Why, I'm disappointed in you, Mo Wren. I thought you were the historian of Fox Street!"

"I know she had a husband. Who got killed in some kind of terrible accident at some kind of factory." Fell into a vat of boiling sauce at the Chef Boyardee tomato sauce plant. Or doused in molten ore at Republic Steel. Or, if you asked the Baggott boys, it was no accident at all—he was poisoned at his own dinner table, a pinch of arsenic in his mashed potatoes every night, till he keeled over onto the floor and she collected his million-dollar life insurance policy.

"In fact," said Da, "it was a car accident."

Mo sank back in her chair.

"Overnight she became a widow alone with a baby

boy. Walter Henry Junior. His eyes were like little chips of sky. Next to Monette, he was the smartest child on the street."

Da chuckled, but then her fanning slowed. Across the street, Starchbutt had sat down in one of her porch chairs and folded her hands in her lap. She couldn't possibly hear what Da was saying, yet she stared as if mesmerized. As if she couldn't wait to hear the end of the story, either.

"After her husband died, Gertrude started getting seriously peculiar. People stayed away from her." Da raised her fan like she wished she had something to swat. "Walter Junior was such a good son! I can't tell you how many black eyes and bloody noses that boy endured, sticking up for his mother when other kids made fun of her."

"But . . . how come her son never visits Starch . . . Mrs. Steinbott?"

"He joined the military directly out of high school." Da pressed O GRAVE, WHERE IS THY VICTORY? to her heart. "He wasn't there but two months before he was killed in a training exercise. Lord give me strength."

Mo collapsed back in her chair. Unpleasant revelations were coming at her one right after another, like a nest of yellow jackets run over by a lawn mower.

"Gertrude's hair turned pure white overnight. She took to that house and barely came out for a year." Da rested the fan in her lap. "That was the year you were born, Mercedes Jasmine. I remember—this is how selfish your Da is. I remember being relieved not to have to see her. I was so happy while she was sunk in grief."

The side door of the Wren house banged, and out zoomed Dottie, clutching a beer bottle in either hand.

"That child's wild as my Monette!" Da clapped a hand over her mouth, but her smile crept out around the edges as Dottie dashed across Mrs. Steinbott's grass (strictly forbidden) and buried her face in a fat yellow rose (penalty of death). "I'll never forget it. The very day after Monette's rose-petal bath, Mr. Walcott planted Gertrude three new bushes. A Martha Washington, a Dinah Shore, and a Purple Contessa." Da nodded. "If I'm not mistaken, we're looking at them right now."

Dottie zigzagged across the street to pick up a cookie at Mrs. Petrone's, then shot out between the parked cars to cross the street again and disappear up the driveway of the A.O.L. House.

"She knows that house is Absolutely Off Limits!"

Mo jumped up. "I gotta go."

"Yes, you may be excused, Mo Wren. But first, answer me this simple question." Attach Da's eyeballs to a drill and Mo would have a hole in her forehead, pronto. "When do you plan to teach that child to look both ways before she crosses?"

"I . . . I . . ." Mo swallowed. "I tried."

"Tried's not good enough!" Da thundered. "You know how those drunk drivers come roaring down this street. Dead end or no. It's not safe!"

"You don't need to tell me that, Da!" The words exploded out of Mo. "I already know!"

You didn't talk to Da that way. Not if you had the sense a goose did. But Mercedes's grandmother didn't scold. Instead she let silence pool there on the porch. She gazed at her toe coffins propped up on the stool. At last she spoke.

"You do your best and then some, Mo. Lord knows what would have become of that handsome, foolish father of yours without your help!" Her hands fumbled with the fan. With a sorry little shock, Mo realized it was true: Da still wasn't strong, and maybe never would be again.

"But I worry about that sister of yours!" Her voice was too small. "Every last one of us does. If anything ever happened to her, well, I can't even think." She touched her throat.

"Nothing's going to happen to her." Mo cupped Da's shoulder. "I give you my pledge. I swear it on a mountain of Bibles. Don't even *think* it, Da!" She swallowed. "Don't think too much, okay?"

"Excuse me." Mercedes's face was pale. "But I refuse to sit here one more second." She jumped up. "Talk about manners—when's she going to learn some?"

Mo and Da looked across the street. Starchbutt stared back.

"She looks at me like she wishes I'd disappear! Like I'm some nightmare she can't wake up from."

"Some people," Da began, then corrected herself. "All of us have our own way of looking at life. Some like things tidy and predictable—isn't that right, Mo Wren?"

"What?"

Da didn't bother to reprimand her for this breach of manners. "On the other hand, some of us have had too much experience of life's mess to hold with that kind of view. Mercedes, Mo, pay attention now. Every person you pass on the street, or wait behind in a line, or see sitting alone on her porch—every one is summoning up the courage for some battle, whether you can see it or not. She jests at scars that never felt a wound!"

Even if Mo's head had been clear, she was pretty sure she wouldn't have known what that meant. She edged toward the step.

"I'm far from the best role model," Da said. "But try to be kind. You never know what you have in common with another person."

Mercedes gaped. "The only thing she and I have in common is we both suck in oxygen. Unless she runs on poison gas, which wouldn't surprise me."

Da sat back, looking worn-out. Over her head, Mercedes rolled her eyes at Mo.

"Um, I better go," Mo said.

Poof!

THE SPARROWS, enjoying their morning dust bath beneath the old lilac, whirled up in an indignant cloud as Mo ran down the steps. The letter was soft and squishy in her sweaty hand. As she ran down the street, Mo tried to imagine her father shouting with outrage, ripping it into a hundred shreds, and flushing it down the toilet.

But as excellent as her imagination was, it failed.

At the end of the street, the Green Kingdom rustled in the late-morning breeze, as if trying to shake off the dust that coated its leaves. On a normal summer afternoon, you could hear the head-over-heels rush of the stream all the way from up here, but today the only sound was the hiss of those leaves.

Mrs. Steinbott with a dead son! Could that be who she was knitting for, like a crazy old lady in a horror movie? So many people on Fox Street were missing things, permanent and otherwise.

1. Mrs. Steinbott: her son.
2. Da: her husband and daughter. Not to mention her toes.
3. Mercedes: her hair.
4. Mo: _____.

Mo, too.

The grass around the beat-up, boarded-up A.O.L. House grew so high, it covered the FOR SALE sign— wait a minute. The FOR SALE sign was gone! The Baggotts must have stolen it. The sign had been there nearly a year, ever since the last people had moved away. A family with two little girls. The older one would ride her bike up and down the street no-handed, grinning. One day they were there, and the next gone. Vanished in the night, skipping out on their rent. *Poof!* As if they'd never existed.

That was how fast a life could change. The blink of

an eye. The turn of a head. Change could come barreling down on you, out of nowhere, without warning, humongous and stupid and unstoppable. While you were just stepping off the curb of a street called Paradise, humming maybe, thinking about your daughter waiting for you back home, beneath the plum tree. Thinking ice cream. Thinking strawberry, your daughter's favorite? Or pistachio, your husband's? How about some of both?

Poof! Just like that. The beat of a heart. She unsquished the letter and looked it over once more. She imagined her father getting a beer, sitting down, reading it through once, then again. Tugging on his cap, rubbing his jaw. Home Plate. The words appeared in cartoon bubbles over his head. Good Food, Good Friends, Good Times.

A down payment on my own place, he'd think. At last! He could make his longtime dream come true. Leave this street behind, start over, just like Monette.

Before her brain could manufacture one more troublesome thought, she ripped the letter in half. That felt so good, she ripped and ripped till a pile of confetti lay at her feet. She scooped that up, climbed over the guardrail, and, balanced on the edge of the world, scattered the pieces far and wide.

The first time in her life Mo Wren had ever littered. Not to mention destroyed someone else's property.

Necessary evil, whispered a voice inside her.

"What you doing?"

Mo whirled around. Dottie spied out from the tall grass.

"What . . . what are *you* doing? You absolutely know that place is Absolutely Off Limits!"

"Playing foxes." She patted down the tall grass, and Mo saw the two beer bottles nestled in her lap. "See our nest?"

"Foxes live in dens!"

"The house is so lonesome. It thinks nobody likes it."

Which made Mo think of Mrs. Steinbott, sitting on her porch all alone, husband and son gone, which somehow made hot tears spurt up into her eyes. She wiped her eyes with the palm of her hand.

Being a thinker was a various thing. Sometimes you felt like a turtle, with a nice, private built-in place to shelter. Other times it was like having a bucket stuck on your head, making the world clang and echo and never stop.

Magic Feather

A MONSTER BOILER, a million times bigger than the one in the basement of Mo's school—that's what the world had turned into. Mo's T-shirt plastered itself to her back. Her curls clenched like fists. Still no rain—not in the sky, not in the forecast, not anywhere. This week, the city had declared an unnecessary-use ban. Watering your grass or washing your car earned you a citation, and every night Mr. Wren came home more disgusted. People were furious! All day long they phoned the water department, complaining. They opened hydrants, wasting thousands of gallons. Was it his fault the blankety-blank sky refused to open? Was it his fault it was taking so long to repair and replace downtown's decrepit, century-old pipes? Yesterday, on his lunch hour, he had stopped for a beer, just minding his own thirsty business after working outside all morning in ninety-degree heat, and some guy had started haranguing him about how municipal employees were lazy and overpaid.

If only Mo had been there! She'd have told that guy a thing or two.

She wished she could water the plum tree again. Its leaves were droopy, the unripe plums falling *plunk plunk* in the dry grass. But how could the daughter of a water department employee violate the ban? Would that qualify as a necessary evil?

Sipping warm, syrupy Tahitian Treat, which somehow only made them thirstier, she and Mercedes languished in the Den, watching Dottie fasten a piece of string to a broken branch with approximately a hundred knots.

"I'm going to go fix a nutritious dinner. Da needs to eat better." But Mercedes didn't move. In the two weeks she'd been here, her bald head had grown a little cap of cinnamon-colored moss. Every day she wore a new outfit, as if she'd brought a magic, bottomless suitcase. Sometimes when Mo turned up in her standard baggy shorts and another Tortilla Feliz team T-shirt, Mercedes rabbited her nose. Mo pretended not to notice.

"Last night I baked corn bread, but the house got so hot I thought the furniture would melt. That old air conditioner doesn't do squat!"

Breathing heavily with her effort, Dottie began to fasten the string to the other end of the branch.

"Three-C called this morning. Somebody needs to explain to him that he's never going to be my real dad, not to mention being a dad doesn't require knowing every single minuscule fact about your child's life." Mercedes slid Mo a sideways look. "Your dad's living proof, right?"

Mercedes knew that Mo had destroyed the Letter. She also knew Mo did not exactly feel great about it, so did she have to bring it up?

"He would just have torn it up himself," Mo said. "I saved him the trouble."

Dottie gnawed the end of a green twig. For someone who ate so much candy, her teeth were surprisingly strong.

"Right," Mercedes agreed. "I'm just saying—"

"Watch this!" Dottie positioned her contraption at arm's length. Fitting the tip of the chewed-up twig to the string, she arched her back, aimed at the sky, and let fly. The twig made a graceful loop-the-loop and landed at her feet. Dottie scowled, picked up the stick, and tried again. And again.

"Dottie, if you don't mind my asking, what do you think you're doing?"

"Bringing the rain!"

Mercedes's face softened. "Did Da read you that book? That was one of my favorites. Kapiti Plain, where it hasn't rained so long, all the crops are shriveling up and the animals are dying, so this guy finds an eagle feather and makes an arrow and—"

"And he shoots the clouds and the rain comes pouring down!" Dottie slapped her forehead. "I forgot the feather—no wonder." She charged off, dry brush crackling beneath her feet.

"At least I don't have a little sister." Mercedes stood up. "Things could be much, much worse." She dusted off her beautiful black jeans. "Da still gets tired by afternoon. I have to make sure she takes her rest. Not to mention takes her pills and rubs the ointment on her feet." Mercedes counted off her duties on her long fingers. "Three-C says she should have recovered from the surgery by now. He says if she lived with us, she'd be seriously healthier." She heaved a sigh. "I'm going."

When Mercedes was gone, Mo tidied up the Den. Every summer till now, Da had fussed over Mercedes as if she were Queen of the Nile. Now it was Mercedes's turn to be the caretaker. No wonder she was a little grumpy and thoughtless. Not to say coldhearted.

Mo set off to fetch Dottie.

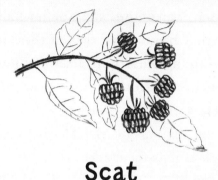

Scat

NOT THAT SHE CALLED her little sister's name. Not yet.

Clumsy human that she was, Mo struggled to keep upright as she made her way down toward the stream. *Vulpes vulpes* had exquisite balance! When a fox ran—and it could run very, very fast—its tracks traced a single true line. Light and swift, a red fox barely dented the ground with its tracks.

Mo tripped over a sticking-up root, tilted backward, landed on her butt, and slid downhill, digging in her heels just in time to prevent scraping her shin against a rusty fender. Flat on her back, dumb as a turkey on a platter.

But then, as she lay there, something began to happen. Slowly, gently, as if she were dreaming with her eyes open, Mo sensed she was no longer alone. The air turned beamy, the rays of the sun weaving themselves into a beautiful quilt. It floated over her, tucked itself in around her. Aah. How safe she felt. Something was watching over her.

The fox, her fox, was nearby. Mo just knew it.

She held as still as she could.

Still as a stone.

Waiting.

Still as a root.

Waiting.

Till at last, with a sigh, she stood back up. She brushed off her backside and broke the woods' stubborn silence.

"Dottie!"

The only answer was the squawk of a jay. The wildflowers drooped. The leaves curled in limp cylinders. As Mo made her way downhill, the angle of the slope sharpened, turning stony and treacherous just before it gave way to the pebbled banks of the stream. Dottie was not allowed down here, period, but she was triple not allowed near the water.

"I know you hear me!"

What if she didn't? How long since Dottie had left the Den? How long had Mo lain there, waiting? She couldn't be sure.

The lip of the ravine was all shale, stacked neatly as a high stone wall. The only way down was to jump, and Mo did, landing in slick mud. Most summers the stream brimmed from bank to bank, from here to where the land sloped up again, then flattened out to become the Metropark. Normally it was wide enough for a stone to take three or four skips across it, but this year it had dwindled down to a measly trickle.

If it didn't rain soon, what would the fox find to drink? By now she probably had kits, who'd be thirsty and depending on her.

"Dorothea Wren!" Mo scanned the edges of the water, and sure enough, a trail of small footprints led straight in. "You're really going to get it now!"

The Metropark was vast, acres and acres of dark woods. Beyond that lay the ball fields, where on weekdays the kinds of strangers anybody would have the sense to avoid—anybody but Dottie—hung out and smoked and sold stuff. And then there were the parking lots where teenagers loved to drink beer and squeal their tires and not look where they were going at fifty miles per hour.

Mo splashed across the stream. She staggered through a patch of wild raspberries, the prickers catching at her shorts and scratching her legs. She had one more fleeting thought of the fox, who'd enjoy those juicy berries. But then thoughts of everything except Dottie fell away. Spruce and hemlock grew here, tall dark trees that blocked the sky and made her shiver. Imagine if you were barely bigger than a fire hydrant. Imagine how confusing it would all be then.

Why hadn't she gone after Dottie right away, instead of lying there so long, waiting for something that never came? Stupid, stupid!

"Dottie!" The two syllables echoed as if flung off the edge of a cliff or against the walls of a cavern. "Dot . . . teeee!"

If anything ever happened to that child . . .

It won't. I swear on a mountain of Bibles.

The trees began to thin out, and now Mo glimpsed pavement. She ran forward, coming out on a sparkling asphalt desert. No cars. No people. Nothing moved. Two large Dumpsters hulked side by side, like the last things left on Earth.

Mo cupped her hands over her mouth, drew her breath up from her belly, and shouted. "DOTTIE

66

WREN! WHERE ARE YOU?"

A mirage. A hallucination. A rust-colored animal poked up from inside the far Dumpster. Mo froze, her heart beating up in her ears.

"It's a mama! Her name's Georgene." Dottie waved a brown bottle.

"I will kill you," cried Mo. "I will decapitate you and use your head for a bowling ball! I will . . . How the heck did you get in there?"

However she'd managed, it must have been easier than getting out. That entailed Mo catching her when she scrambled over the side, odoriferous and soaking—she'd managed to fall into the stream after all. Mo wasn't even a quarter through her lecture when a car tore into the parking lot, made a few wild circles, ejected a stream of empty beer cans, laid down rubber, and sped back out, music up so loud it thumped in her own chest like a second, demented heart.

"Don't you see how dangerous . . . you're so . . . so . . ." Mo slumped against the repugnant Dumpster. "What were you thinking? Never mind. I know you don't think."

Dottie rummaged in her thicket of hair, as if the answer hid in there. Cheer suffused her grimy little face, and she plucked out a brilliant blue feather.

"I found it! Now I can make it rain, and Daddy won't have to work so hard."

Mo plucked a slimy potato peel from her sister's shoulder. "That's nice of you, all right, but magic . . . it doesn't always work."

Dottie was quiet for a long moment. "I wish he was happy. I wish he wasn't always so doomy."

"Gloomy."

"Yeah." Dottie leaned her revolting self into Mo's stomach and yawned. "Can we go home now?"

Mo was far from sure of the way back, but Dottie followed at her heels, trusting as a puppy.

"Dot, don't tell Daddy you got lost."

"Okay." She yawned again. "Did I get lost?"

They must be headed the right direction, because here was the same raspberry patch. Setting down Georgene, Dottie picked with both hands, smearing her mouth and chin rosy.

"You'll get a bellyache." Mo's warning was only half-hearted. Dottie never got bellyaches.

Mo sat down, and something partly hidden beneath the matted, dead leaves caught her eye. At first glance it was a mess of crushed berries. Leaning closer, she realized it was a ruby-colored pile of droppings, the size of a small dog's. But what dog would eat raspberries?

Not a dog. But a *Vulpes vulpes*.

"Poor Mo." Dottie patted her shoulder with a juicy hand. "She's smiling at a poop pile."

"Not poop," whispered Mo. "Scat."

"Scat cat!" Dottie shoved in more berries.

Was this the sign she'd been waiting for? The sign that, if you were patient, if you believed hard enough and held on tight, good things would come? The world would right itself, and all, all would be well?

Mo put a berry on her tongue and crushed it against the roof of her mouth. Sweet, sharp, warm juice shot out. Deliciousness spurted all through her.

The Letter, Part 2

BACK HOME, Mr. Wren sprawled in front of the TV, where Mo saw at a glance that the Indians were down by five runs. The scent of earthworms drifted off him, and his fingernails were earth caked.

"Where you girl-illas been? What'd I tell you about being home here by five?" Without waiting for an answer, he hoisted himself off the couch. They could hear the refrigerator opening, the top popping on a can. "Don't listen to me," he said, coming back into the room. "I was underground eight hours today. My brain's clogged with dirt." He pointed at Georgene. "Nice score." Mr. Wren only drank beer from cans, but still he took an interest.

"I brought you a feather," Dottie said, holding it out. But Mr. Wren turned away to snap off the TV.

"Bunch of losers!" He trudged into the hallway and wrestled with the front door, which always stuck in the humidity. "This bleepin' hole!"

"Hey, it's the world's best house! You always said so."

"Yeah, well. Every frog praises his own pond." Mr. Wren yanked the door open and stepped outside.

Dottie hung her head. "That feather's not no magic."

"Don't worry." Mo stroked her hair. "We don't need magic. Everything's going to be okay."

Mo woke the next morning to hear her father on the phone, calling in sick. He made his voice weak and hoarse, claiming fever. By the time she came downstairs, he and Dottie were busy in the kitchen. Dottie was in charge of toast, and the stack was already about a foot high. His hair, still wet from his shower, curled in shiny black parentheses all over his head. Mr. Wren, who could not carry a tune in a bucket yet loved to sing, was belting out "Please Please Me" when a knock sounded at the side door.

"Bernard!" Mr. Wren opened the door wide. "You smell the bacon or what?"

"I know that front door of yours sticks in this kind of weather, so I moseyed myself up the side." Bernard stepped into the kitchen, swinging his mail sack off his shoulder and onto a chair. Mr. Wren was getting an extra plate, but Bernard shook his head. "I gotta say, this is the eatingest street on my route! Already had some of Da's biscuits and a killer cup of espresso at Mrs. Petrone's. It's a shame, but I can't eat me one more bite. Day off?"

Mr. Wren tapped his temple. "Mental health."

Bernard pulled a rubber-banded bundle of envelopes from his sack and handed one to Mr. Wren, who frowned at the return address.

"I pay my taxes. I'm up on the mortgage. What the bleep's this?"

Bernard frowned, holding out a pen. "Looks to me like part two."

"Then I missed part one."

Bernard raised a brow in the direction of Mo, who bent her face over her eggs.

"Sign right there." Taking the receipt, Bernard swung his gray bag back up on his shoulder. "Maybe opportunity's come knocking."

"Opportunity comes knocking on Fox Street, it's got the wrong address, Bernard."

"Remind me to stop here first next time." Bernard flicked Mo another questioning look. "Well, you all have a fine day now."

As Mr. Wren tore open the letter, Mo busied herself clearing the table. She was scrubbing the frying pan when he gave a long, low whistle.

"Either this Buckman's wiggity or it's our lucky day."

"Buckman!" Dottie ran around the table flapping her arms like chicken wings. *Buck buck buck!*

Mr. Wren refolded the letter, looking thoughtful. "What do you say to a trip to Paradise, Little Speck?" He put the letter in his pocket and pulled on his base-ball cap.

Wiping her hands on a dish towel, Mo struggled to make her face innocent and her voice casual.

"What's up, Daddy?"

"We'll soon find out."

"Can I get a donut at Abdul's?" Dottie was already begging.

"Who's Buck . . . Buck Man, did you say?"

"Like the man said, we'll soon find out." He downed the last of his coffee. "A couple of weeks ago, I stopped into Paradise Realty just for the heck of it. I told Marcie—you know Marcie? She wears those suits that look like they're made to withstand kryptonite?

I told her, give me a ring next time some millionaire comes in wanting a nice little place with a view of the park. I love making Marcie laugh."

He hoisted Dottie onto his wide shoulders. "Wait'll she sees this letter—she'll bust a gut. Hey." His brow furrowed. "Why so thoughtful, Mojo?"

"Who, me?"

"You're off babysitting duty." He tickled the bottom of Dottie's bare foot, then dug out his wallet and laid a ten-dollar bill on the table. "Treat Ferrari to an ice cream. Go to the pool or see a movie. That's an order."

He wrestled open the door, Dottie ducking her head. "Toodle-oo!" she cried.

"Daddy! She's in her pajamas! She needs shoes!"

Bam!

Mo wiped the ketchup off the scarred wooden table, put the milk away, and went upstairs to get dressed. The feeling that something very bad was about to happen—that it had, in fact, already started happening—made every step an effort. Was this what it was like just before you died, when your life flashed before your eyes? People said "flashed," but time would have to crawl in order for you to review your whole life. Why, a single day alone would take several minutes, and if you added up all the hundreds and hundreds of days . . .

Of course you probably didn't review every single day. Just a few moments, maybe. Like a highlights reel. But how could you ever pick which moments? Most of your life would be left behind, like the A.O.L. House, abandoned and hurt, sure you didn't care about it.

Mo pulled on her shorts. Sometimes her thoughts got more knotty than the Wild Child's hair. Sometimes being a thinker led her round and round and right back where she'd started. Only dizzy.

Still moving in slow motion, she walked down the driveway, pausing to admire Mrs. Steinbott's roses. Somehow, even in the drought, the flowers were flourishing. Mo's favorites were just coming into bud. Cream colored, flame tipped—by the time those flowers opened all the way, they'd be big as a newborn's head.

"Pssst!"

Mrs. Steinbott peered down from her porch, her face a pink knot.

"You!" She crooked a bloodless finger. "Come here."

Shocked, Mo looked around. No one else in sight.

"Are you a moron? Come here this instant!"

Stink Bomb

MO HAD NEVER, in her entire lifetime, which as everyone knew had been spent entirely on Fox Street, climbed Mrs. Steinbott's porch steps. Not that she'd ever wanted to. The Baggott boys had, dozens of times, depositing a sack of dog poop or a dead mouse, ringing the doorbell and running for their cowardly, shrivel-brained lives. The Jehovah's Witness ladies had, and a cookie-selling Girl Scout from two streets over who didn't know any better, but nobody, nobody, was ever *invited* up those four gleaming white steps. Till now.

"Invited" was probably too polite a word.

"That's far enough!"

Starchbutt swung her hand up like a traffic cop.

"You're going to Walcotts'. You go there every day."

"That's right, Mrs. Steinbott. I do." Mo attempted to make her voice pleasant. Maybe, who knew, they could have a little chat. Maybe she could ask Mrs. Steinbott why she stared at Mercedes that way and, if possible, could she cut it out? Immediately? "Mercedes Walcott is my best friend. She and I—"

"Take this." Mrs. Steinbott picked up a box lying on a low wicker table and thrust it toward Mo. The box was entombed in pink tissue paper held together with at least half a roll of tape.

"How nice," Mo said, still working on the pleasant tone. "Who's this nice present for, may I ask?"

"You know!" Mrs. Steinbott sputtered. How skinny she was! A good wind would knock her flat. She narrowed her eyes. "You didn't know, did you?"

"Well, it's been a delight. I hope we can do this again." Mo sped down the stairs. "Not!" she added as she crossed the street.

She found Mercedes, who refused to sit on the front porch anymore, lying on Da's couch, talking on her cell.

"I know I promised." When she saw Mo, she held

up a finger and went back to the call. "She's at a doctor's appointment right now. The church van took her—she's fine. She takes her insulin and . . . Mom, if you're so concerned, why don't you just come up here yourself and . . . I'm not being fresh!" She rolled her eyes at Mo. "Yes, I got the money. Tell him I said . . ." Here Mercedes's voice choked up as if a boa constrictor had her by the throat. "Tell him I said thanks, dude." More eye rolling. "Dude? Dad? It's one vowel!" She put her hand over the phone. "She should be grateful I didn't say dud." She spoke back into the phone. "Excuse me?"

Mo set down the present and wandered around the living room, dusting furniture with the hem of her T-shirt and straightening piles of newspapers. Da did the daily crossword, in ink of course, but hadn't gotten to it in a while. A stack of puzzles going back as far as December moldered on an end table. Mo took a bouquet of flowers that had seen better days and dumped it off the side of the porch. When she came back in, Mercedes still lay on the sofa, an arm flung over her eyes, her ultrasensitive nose twitching.

"What is that repulsive smell?" she asked.

Mo set Mrs. Steinbott's package on Mercedes' chest.

"Your secret admirer sent it."

"The Queen of the Night?" Mercedes sat up. "What if it's a bomb?"

"I don't hear any ticking."

Mo sat beside Mercedes while she undid the zillion layers of paper and tape. What could be so precious? Inside was a box and, inside that, more paper.

"This is creeping me out." Mercedes pushed it into Mo's hands. "You open it."

"Thanks so much." Mo extracted a little jar of pink crystals, its label yellowed and peeling at the edges. "Imperial Deluxe Rose-Scented Bubble Bath," she read.

"Great!" Mercedes flung herself backward on the couch. "Now she's telling me I need a bath. What next?"

"I may be wrong, but I think she's trying to be nice."

Mercedes's eyes grew wide. "I only take showers! I haven't taken a bath since I was four years old! She knows nada about me! Negative zip!"

"It's the thought that counts. Right?"

"Look at that ancient jar! It could be from Pompeii. Crudsicles!" Mercedes threw an arm over her eyes. "I'm besieged by adults on all sides."

Mo thought of the letter her father had just gotten, and how he'd catapulted out the door to the realty company. If she told Mercedes about that, it would prove Mercedes wasn't the only one with problems brewing.

But what if it was the new, heartless Mercedes who answered? What if, instead of sympathizing, she replied, "Why are you so surprised? He'd do anything to quit the water department—you know it as well as I do."

"You're exaggerating," Mo said. "It's not that bad."

Mercedes lowered her arm and peered at Mo. "It's not that good, either. But you refuse to admit it."

"Guess what?" The sudden urge to tell Mercedes about the fox scat shot up inside Mo like her own personal geyser. "I found something I've been looking for a long time."

"What?"

Mo hesitated again. What if Mercedes wrinkled her hyperactive nose and demanded to know what, precisely, did a poop pile have to do with anything? Mo clutched the ancient jar of bath crystals. The truth was, she could no longer predict how her best friend would react to things. She couldn't count on Mercedes to say the thing she most needed to hear.

Not to mention, what if all she'd discovered was the poop of a weird dog with a taste for raspberries?

"What?" repeated Mercedes.

Mo stood up. "Umm, nothing."

Mercedes lowered her window-shade arm again. "If I didn't know how much you hate secrets, I'd swear you were keeping one from me."

"Me? Secrets? Ha ha."

"Three-C sent me money. Want to do something?"

Mo was about to say her father had given her ten dollars when Mercedes pulled two twenties from her pocket.

"We could take the bus to the mall," Mercedes suggested.

"The mall?" When they had some money, they usually toured the aisles of the E-Z Dollar, then got pop and chips at Abdul's Market. "We never go to the mall."

"And we can never do something we never do."

"I mean . . ."

"Never mind. I'll just lie here all day, perfecting my sarcophagus imitation."

Hurt, Mo turned toward the door.

"Please," added Mercedes, "could you kindly take that stink bomb with you?"

Stepping onto Da's porch, the first thing Mo saw was Mrs. Steinbott standing on her lawn clutching her big pruning shears. What if she concluded Mo was stealing the wonderful present for herself? She might call the police, which she regularly did on the Baggott boys. Or attempt to stab Mo through the heart with those colossal shears, the way she'd once dispatched a UPS driver who got the wrong address. People said.

Mo slid the pink jar into the top of her shorts and pulled her T-shirt over it. As she crossed the street, Pi Baggott rumbled up on his board.

"Wazzup." His skin was a map of scars and scrapes. His full name was Pisces, but instead of a fish, he longed to be a bird. No matter how often he wiped out, he was back on that board, trying to fly.

Speaking of boards.

"You got a new one," she said.

Pi was the kind of person who always had something in his hands, something he was fixing or improving. While Mo could never stop considering and wondering and stewing over life's endless complications, Pi inhabited a fret-free zone. Not that he was thoughtless. Just that the part of him that did his thinking seemed to be located in his hands, not his brain.

"I found it down the ravine. I can't believe what people throw away. All it needed was new wheels."

He flipped it over to show her how he'd removed the axle nuts and replaced the old wheels with shining new ones. He'd scraped off the old decals, too, and sanded it smooth as glass.

"It's better than new," Mo said.

"Try it." He set it at her feet and held out his hand. "I'll hold that."

"What?"

"Whatever you're smuggling under your shirt."

By now Mrs. Steinbott was beckoning impatiently from her porch.

"You!" she called. "Get over here!"

"Hey," said Pi. "Is that bloodsucker bothering you? Want me to hose her for you?"

"It's okay."

"Just let me know." He jumped back on his board. "Or if you ever want to borrow my board."

"Skateboarding's not for me."

Pi looked puzzled. "How do you know that?" He rolled away, popping a smooth, sweet ollie.

"You!" repeated Mrs. Steinbott. She leaned over her porch railing. Mo crossed her arms over the bulge beneath her shirt. "What did she say?"

"She said . . . wow. She'd never seen the like."

Mrs. Steinbott continued to fix Mo with an expectant

look, as if there must be more.

"She said . . ." For some unearthly reason, Mo longed to tell her crazy neighbor whatever it was she longed to hear. If only she could guess what that might be. From the foot of the steps she gazed up while Mrs. Steinbott gazed down, the two of them yearning toward each other, their longings crisscrossing above the glorious, indifferent roses.

"She liked it," Mrs. Steinbott prompted.

Mo clutched the jar with one hand and slid the other behind her back, crossing her fingers. "She really did."

Mrs. Steinbott nodded. Exactly the answer she'd been looking for. Settling back in her chair, she picked up her knitting needles and commenced clicking away, her eyes on Da's front porch, as if it were an empty stage and she were waiting for the play to begin.

Magic Hands

"Mo!"

Mrs. Petrone, power-walking past, paused to unhook the earbuds of her iPod. She was always testing new beauty products on herself, and today her hair was gelled up into a sort of picket fence. In the heat, her round face was shiny and pink as her track pants.

"Isn't it about time for a visit to my shop?" The way she eyed Mo's hair, Mo knew it wasn't really a question.

The next thing Mo knew, she was in Mrs. Petrone's kitchen, which smelled like strong coffee and coconut shampoo, not to mention was delectably air-conditioned. For as long as Mo could remember,

Mrs. Petrone had cut her hair. Her cheery kitchen had shelves full of cookbooks and a special album of cards and letters from the grateful families of people whose hair and makeup she'd styled at the House of Wills. "You made Grandma resemble an angel," one letter said. "We hardly recognized Uncle George, and that is a total compliment," read another.

"Business is slow," she told Mo, lining up her bottles and combs and scissors. "People don't die in the summer if they can help it. Winter, that's a different story."

When she washed your hair, Mrs. P was more or less a hypnotist. You never had to be nervous she'd dig into your scalp, or tug too hard, or do anything but massage firmly yet gently, so before you knew it, she'd thrown you into a sort of trance.

"*Bella, bella*," crooned Mrs. Petrone. "You've got the best hair on the street—don't tell anyone I said so."

She didn't ask Mo how she wanted her hair cut. She knew—not too short, not too long, just right. Mo's eyes drifted shut. The chair cupped her like a big, warm hand. Mrs. Petrone talked and talked, her voice a lullaby. Murmuring how when she was a young girl, her hair was so long she could sit on it, how every night her mother brushed it one hundred strokes, how those were some of the happiest moments of her life.

"That was a lifetime ago, but I remember it like it happened yesterday," she said. "But oh, don't ask me where I put my keys!"

She set down her scissors and pulled the lid off a big red tin on the counter. A plate of golden pizzelles, dusted with sugar, appeared on the table in front of Mo. The cookies were thin and crisp, fragrant with vanilla. All at once, Mo felt sick.

"Go on—I remember how you like them."

But here Mrs. Petrone remembered all wrong. Mo could no more eat a pizzelle than a fried worm. Just the sight of one filled her ears with the terrible wrenching wail of sirens.

Sirens! They blared on Paradise all the time. Mo had hardly noticed them that summer afternoon. She'd been too happy, thinking of ice cream, imagining her mother's smile when she saw the rocks Mo had collected.

That was almost the worst part. It was too terrible to think that she'd heard those sirens and never guessed. Heard them and ignored them, blissful and ignorant as a baby. That afternoon, someone drew a cruel line down the center of the world and left Mo on the wrong side.

Now she gripped the arms of her chair.

"Dottie's the one who loves pizzelles," she managed to say.

"Dottie looks more like your mother every day. That head of hair, wild and red as a little fox!"

Mo couldn't remember how she and Dottie had wound up at Mrs. Petrone's that afternoon—had their father brought them here, after the hospital called? Had Mrs. Petrone come and fetched them, squashing Dottie to her big, cushiony chest? Sometimes Mo thought that, if only he'd brought them to Da's instead, things would have turned out differently. Da would have warded It off, she'd never have allowed It to cross her threshold.

But Da's husband had died. Her daughter had gone away and not come back. Four of her toes had wound up in the hospital incinerator. Maybe even Da couldn't have protected them.

"You bring that little sister over, and between the two of us we'll hold her down and give her a nice cut."

Dottie hadn't understood. She'd watched cartoons till her eyes fell out and eaten one pizzelle after another, scattering sugary golden crumbs everywhere. Mo had sat frozen on Mrs. Petrone's scratchy living-room couch, the pockets of her shorts heavy with stones.

Because Mo and her mother were going to paint those stones Mo had collected, turn them into bugs and flowers and tiny people. They were going to do it in the backyard, beneath the plum tree. Afterward they were going to sit at the wooden table in the kitchen, the one printed with the secret language of all their dinners together, and eat the ice cream her mother had gone to buy.

That day Mo had sat perfectly still on the Petrone couch, eyes on the door, certain Mr. Wren would burst in any minute to fetch them home. Maybe their mother would have a big Band-Aid on her head. Or her arm in a sling. *That's what I get for my daydreaming!* She'd laugh and they'd hug, but carefully, in case she was still sore.

Mo had sat on the couch and waited. Her foot fell asleep. Her nose itched, her empty belly ached, Dottie tipped over sideways, sound asleep and drooling on her shoulder. But Mo forced herself to stay still. Still as a stone herself. Because if she froze her own self, she could make the rest of the world stand still, too. If things couldn't go forward, nothing bad could happen.

When at last her father had come, Mo jumped up from the couch, but she'd forgotten about her rock-heavy pockets and lost her balance, tipping over backward. It was exactly like some invisible bully, big and stupid as a furniture truck, had plowed into her.

She should have held still. Still as a stone!

Now Mrs. Petrone was pouring Mo a glass of milk.

"You're too pale. You need to eat! My mother always made her pizzelles with anise. You know anise, it's like licorice? I never could stomach it. Chin up, please. I remember . . ."

Their father had put his arms around her and Dottie and lifted them, one in each arm, as if they were made of feathers. How strong he was! Even then, never more than then. Back home he took them both into the big bed, where they slept burrowed against him.

". . . though that I'd just as soon forget!" Mrs. Petrone tossed her head and gave her hearty laugh. What had she just said? Mo had lost track. "But what can you do? Some memories you cherish and some break your heart. We don't get to choose. Our memories choose us."

With that she whisked the beauty cape from Mo's shoulders and handed her the mirror.

"Look what a beauty you are!" she exulted. "Your father's eyes, dark as midnight! Ah, I remember how your mother wept when I gave you your first haircut! You kept patting her arm, saying, 'I don't hurt,

Mama!'" She crushed Mo, mirror and all, against her embarrassing chest. "Let me wrap some pizzelles for you to take home."

Before she knew it, Mo found herself back out on the sidewalk, her clipped hair lifting in the breeze. The foil of the wrapped-up cookies glinted in the sunlight.

She'd never heard the story of her first haircut before.

Fox Street. Here was where all the memories lived. Up on Da's porch. In Mrs. Petrone's kitchen.

Most of all in the Wren house. They snuggled in every corner, rode the air itself. They hovered, just out of sight but near, watching over you with wise, almond-shaped eyes.

Not a single car or person was in sight in this stifling heat, yet Mo looked both ways before she crossed the street. Walking up her driveway, she heard Mrs. Steinbott's radio, but in place of the angry voices that usually raged twenty-four seven, music spilled out. Mo stopped, astonished, to listen. A woman's voice, smooth as cream, sang about long-lost love. A skinny, hopeful voice warbled along.

The Plot Thickens

MR. WREN CALLED IN SICK the next day, too. He whistled as he dressed, not in his uniform but in a good blue shirt.

"Help On-the-Dot get dressed, could you?" he asked Mo. "Shoes, underwear, the whole deal. The Wrens are taking a trip downtown."

"Cool!" Mo faked enthusiasm, even as her radar for surprises began to beep. "What for?"

He slipped a necktie under his collar. A necktie! Mr. Wren pulled the knot tight and stepped back to look in the mirror. He was dazzlingly handsome. Could she really look like him?

"I'm taking a meeting with the illustrious Buck-meister."

Mo put her hands to her own throat.

"Can . . . can Mercedes come with us?"

"Porsche? She's family! But tell her to move it. I can't be late."

Mo grabbed a pair of underwear, a top and shorts that actually matched, shoes and socks, and laid them out in a row on Dottie's bed. She threatened her little sister with a gruesome death if she didn't get dressed immediately, then raced across the street.

She found Da sitting at her kitchen table, where the pill bottles clustered like a miniature plastic forest. One by one Da sorted the capsules and tablets into a tray with boxes labeled for each day of the week.

"There's small choice in rotten apples, Mo Wren." She dropped a big white pill into Thursday and waved the fruit flies off a bowl of bananas. "Old age isn't fun, but it does beat the alternative."

The way fingers can't resist a scab, Mo's eyes drifted down to the floor. In the heat, Da had left off her big black shoes. Instead her feet wore a pair of toeless slippers. *Eeek!* Mo squashed her eyes shut just in time. She clapped her hand over them, for good measure.

"Are you all right, child?"

"It's just a little . . . a little hot in here." Mo inched her fingers down.

"In more ways than one." Da arched a brow. "Am I mistaken, or does Mercedes Jasmine seem especially moody to you?"

"Woo. You said it."

"Just like her mother. Give me strength—that girl could sulk." Da snapped Thursday closed. "It stems from excessive pride. Not that I'd know anything about that. Get yourself a cold drink, go on."

"I'm all right. Where is she?"

"'The quality of mercy is not strained. It droppeth as the gentle rain from heaven.' Give me strength—not *our* Mercey."

"Umm, I'm kind of in a hurry, Da. May I be excused?"

"She's out back. If anyone can cheer her up, it's you, Mo Wren."

Mo crossed the little yard, sending an iridescent pigeon rumpling up from the grass. Mercedes slouched on Da's metal glider, arms crossed, lower lip stuck out at least half a mile.

Mo sat beside her. Back and forth they went, Mercedes's foot thumping off the ground hard. Mo rummaged through her brain, trying to think what it would take to get Mercedes to agree to come down-town. At last she settled on the truth.

"I really need your help. I've got something I can't do myself."

There it was—two sticks rubbed together, sparking a light in Mercedes's eyes. It was the same spark as last summer, when the city closed down the pool's high dive, which Mercedes adored. She and Mo staged a sit-in demonstration, and even though the high dive never reopened, they got their photos in the paper, plus a personal letter of regret from the mayor. The same spark as two summers ago, when Leo Baggott blew off half his finger with a Fourth of July bottle rocket. Mercedes was the one who found it in the grass, and knew to put it in milk and give it to Mrs. Baggott, who fainted dead away. Later Mercedes and Mo held a bake sale, to help pay the medical expenses.

"What's the problem?"

"My dad got a second letter from Buckman."

Mercedes halted the glider with such force, it nearly dislocated Mo's head.

"The plot thickens," Mercedes said.

"Did Da get a letter?"

"No. I've been watching the mail. As far as I can tell, he's targeting your dad."

"My dad's on the way down to meet with him. It's getting serious." Mo swallowed. "I'm afraid he . . . I'm just afraid."

"Let's go."

Skipping the details, they told Da they were headed downtown with Mr. Wren. Da gave Mo an appreciative wink. Mercedes flung open the door, then stopped abruptly.

"What the . . ."

A bucket brimming with roses sat in the middle of the porch. Red roses, white roses, roses the pink of a baby girl's blanket. A trail of scattered petals, like Hansel and Gretel's bread crumbs, led down the front walk and out into the street.

The porch across the street stood empty. But the lace curtain at the front window twitched.

"Rose bubble bath. Rose roses. I guess . . ." Mo remembered Mrs. Steinbott leaning over her porch railing, yearning to hear that Mercedes had appreciated the bubble bath. "She really did," Mo had promised. Not to say lied.

That lace curtain quivered. "I guess she thinks you like roses, Merce."

"Once again proving she doesn't know the first thing about me! Roses make me sneeze."

The scent of those roses was a fragrant river. Lift one to your nose and it flooded you, swept you right off your feet. Mo held one out. "Smell! It's heaven!"

But Mercedes's ridiculously sensitive nose accordioned up, her eyes shut down, her shoulders heaved, and out flew a deafening sneeze.

Beep beep! Mr. Wren was backing the car down the driveway, the side mirror missing Mrs. Steinbott's house by approximately one inch. Dottie waved merrily from the backseat. Just before climbing in, Mo turned and waved to the lace curtain.

On the Case

MR. WREN DROVE ALONG the shore of Lake Erie, beneath a sky heavy with clouds. Far out on the water, whitecaps rolled and broke. Any other time, it would have looked like rain, but this summer, rain was an impossible dream.

He took the long way round, careful not to pass the water-main project. They parked on a side street, in front of a shoe store with a GOING OUT OF BUSINESS sign in the window. Next door was a restaurant plastered with FOR RENT signs. Peering in, you could see tables still set with plates and silverware and plastic flowers in vases.

"Cool," said Dottie, flattening her nose against the glass. "A ghost restaurant."

A scrap of paper blew against Mo's legs.

In the lobby of the building, the elevator wore an OUT OF ORDER sign, so they climbed three flights of stairs. UCKMAN AND BUCKMA read the peeling sign on the door. As they entered, a young woman with a worried, bunched-up face looked up from her desk.

"Mr. Wren, right?"

Mr. Wren grinned his movie-star grin, and Mo could see he was flattered. "How'd you guess?"

"If you ask me," Mercedes muttered, looking around, "they don't exactly get hordes of customers up here."

"Mr. Buckman Senior is expecting you." The secretary bit her bottom lip. "In fact, I better tell him right this minute that you're—"

The door behind her swung open, and a large belly barreled out. Behind it came a man with a broad red face, wearing a tie the yellow of caution tape.

"Mr. Wren! Bob Buckman!" He grabbed Mo's father's hand and pumped it up and down. "I apologize for my assistant keeping you waiting!"

The secretary reddened. "I'm sorry, I—"

"It's so hard to get good help these days." Buckman

said this to Mr. Wren as if it were a great joke.

Mr. Wren frowned. "We just got here."

At the "we," Mr. Buckman noticed the girls for the first time. He swung back around to his secretary.

"Take good care of these children while we confer." He gestured toward his inner office. "This way, please!"

Mr. Wren threw Mo an inquiring look, but when she gave him the thumbs-up, he and Mr. Buckman disappeared through the door, which shut behind them with an emphatic click.

The secretary pulled open a drawer and produced a bag of peppermint patties. "He's mean," said Dottie, helping herself. "You're nice."

Mercedes paced up and down the room—approximately seven paces each way. The carpet was worn, as if lots of people had paced here.

"If you don't mind my asking," she said to the secretary, "are there really two of them?"

The woman smiled for the first time, showing dimples in both cheeks.

"They're clones, only Junior's even stingier. Whoops, did I say that?"

Mo looked out the window, whose sill was speckled with pigeon poop. The clouds still hung heavy and dark.

"And what's their business again?" Mercedes kept her voice cool, as if these were just idle questions to while away this boring time they had to wait

"Developers. They buy and sell. Or, as Mr. B Senior likes to say, they turn things around." She chewed her lip. "Or upside down. Or inside out."

Dottie helped herself to two more chocolates. "He's mean. You're nice."

The secretary unwrapped a patty for herself. "No comment," she said.

"Why do you think he's so interested in a little house on Fox Street?" Mercedes went on.

"It's not so little," Mo couldn't help saying.

The secretary gnawed her bottom lip. Lipstick and chocolate flecked her teeth. "That's confidential information."

The phone rang.

"Yes, Mr. Buckman," said the secretary. "No, Mr. Buckman . . . today? This afternoon? But you specifically said the deadline was . . . Yes, yes, I mean no, no . . ."

Mercedes halted in front of the desk. Time was short. Mr. Wren might be out any minute. She raised her chin, doing her steeple imitation.

"It doesn't make sense that they're so eager to buy

the Wrens' house," she said as soon as the secretary hung up. Her voice was low and calm. Here at last, the Mercedes Mo knew! Loyal. Courageous. Smarter than nine out of ten grown-ups. Mo's ancient love for her friend came rushing back. "I get the feeling something shady's going on. But you don't seem like a shady person to me."

The secretary looked insulted, then pleased, then confused. "I just work here. Do you have any idea how hard jobs are to find?"

Mercedes clasped her hands to her chest. She nodded toward Mo and Dottie.

"They're motherless," she said, and now that calm, cool voice trembled. "A tragedy. They're half orphans."

"Shoot," said the secretary, her face filling with pity. Hey, Mo wanted to burst out. No need to feel sorry for us! Hey! We're perfectly fine! Hold your tears! But Mercedes shot her a look that made her bite her tongue.

"The way it works, B and B acquire homes at market prices. They develop properties that generate much-needed tax income for municipalities." The secretary gave Mo an apologetic look. "But don't worry, they only pursue eminent domain as a last resort."

"Domain? What's that?" demanded Mercedes.

"Whoever has domain over something owns it." She tried to straighten a pile of papers. "In certain extreme situations, the city can exercise ownership over private property."

"What kind of situations?"

"If it's for the good of all."

"That's bogus!" Mo jumped to her feet.

"Is that legal?" Mercedes demanded. "It doesn't sound legal to me."

"Lots of bad stuff is legal!" The secretary swept her hand through the air, knocking over the papers she'd just straightened. "Shoot! The world is full of necessary e—"

"That's not true!" Mo said

"That's not true!" echoed Dottie, slipping a few more patties into her pocket.

The door behind the desk swung open, making the woman jump half out of her skin. Mr. Wren, his tie crooked, came out first, Buckman's big belly following close behind.

"I'll shoot you those figures pronto," he said, clapping Mr. Wren on the shoulder. He beamed at the three girls. "I trust my gal here kept you out of trouble?"

The Thinker, Part 2

"IT'S COMPLICATED," Mr. Wren replied to every question Mo asked. He turned on the radio and hummed along, not saying anything more till he'd edged the car up the driveway, which was so narrow you could touch Mrs. Steinbott's house as you went by, if you were Dottie and dumb enough to want to. He shut off the car but didn't get out. He sat gripping the wheel for a long moment and at last turned around to face the backseat.

"You girls only need to know one thing. Whatever I do is for the good of us all."

This sounded alarmingly familiar. "Like eminent domain?"

"What?" He gave Mo a distracted look, then climbed out of the car. "I need to think."

But instead of thinking, he changed his clothes and went to softball practice. Mercedes had to go help Da, and Dottie threw herself down in front of a hospital-emergency show with the fan blasting directly on her.

That left Mo to do the thinking.

She tried, while sprinkling the plum tree with water she'd saved from Dottie's bath, but all her brain got was static. When she told Dottie she was going out for a little while, her sister didn't take her eyes from the TV screen.

"Give me strength. Ashley's in the hospital. She crashed her car and fell into a compost."

"Do you mean coma, and are you allowed to watch those shows? Don't bother to answer and do not move. I'll be back in a few minutes—I have to check something."

The air was a sponge begging to be wrung out, but the sidewalks and grass were dry as ever. It was late afternoon by now, the day paused between day and evening, Mo's favorite time. She loved to feel the world simmering down, breathing slower. As she slid down the hill into the Green Kingdom, a blue plastic bag fluttered gently, high in a tree. Mo tried, as always, not to make a sound.

She walked up one side of the stream, jumped across, and patrolled the other as far as she could before the brush got too dense, all the while peering at the slick mud. Fox tracks were hard to distinguish from a dog's. Four ovals and a little pad, with sharp, pointy claws. Foxes moved like dancers, so their tracks didn't go as deep as most dogs', but still. Unless you were a real expert, it was hard to tell.

A group of dogs was a pack, of geese a gaggle, of lions a pride. A group of foxes was called an earth. That was perfect, if you asked Mo.

Just before the nettles and weeds grew too thick to penetrate, the stream curved and widened out a bit. Mo squatted to look more closely. The mud was a mishmash of indentations—fat and needle thin, deep or barely a thumbprint, crescents and rays, ovals and lines. A group of something had been here and left behind this record, like a secret language. Another secret language, alongside the one imprinted on the Wren kitchen table.

By this time in summer, kits would be big enough to come out of the den and play. Their mother would still catch all their food, but when she was sure the coast was clear, she'd lead them to water for a drink.

Mo's eyes searched the hillside, looking for a hole. Oh, they were so smart—so foxy! If a den was nearby, it was perfectly camouflaged. Though a fly landed on her knee and a mosquito buzzed in her ear, Mo didn't move. The mother would be watching. She'd be sizing Mo up, deciding whether to trust her or not.

You can. Mo shut her eyes and concentrated, sending her thoughts out into the dusty air. *You can trust me. I promise.*

She kept her eyes shut as long as she could, then slowly opened them.

Nothing. The hillside stared back at her, empty as far as she could see.

Motherless. Mo remembered that dumb-butt secretary's sad-eyed look when Mercedes said that. *Half orphans.*

A gulping sound shook out of her. Mo bit the inside of her cheeks but couldn't stop the tears. How dare that secretary pity them! The thought made Mo furious, which was why she was crying, no other reason. If that secretary felt so sorry for them, why didn't she do something to help? Not that Mo needed any help!

Wait. She swallowed salt, choking back her tears. She'd heard something in the distance. A quick barkish sound, but musical, singing a high-pitched harmony with her crying. There—again! As if trying to tell her something important.

Lift your head. Look around.

And now, wiping her eyes, she saw—what did she see? And how could she have not seen it before?

Just beyond her nose, caught in the thicket, a red-gold tuft glinted in the sun's spotlight. It weighed no more than a snippet lying on Mrs. Petrone's kitchen floor after a haircut. Mo laid it in her palm. The strands of fur were like rough silk, shading from red to creamy white. They were lush and electric at the same time. They felt alive. Like one of Mrs. Steinbott's roses, only more beautiful. Mo closed her fingers around the fur.

The sign she'd been waiting for.

Back home, holding her breath, she set the fur on a bit of dark blue tissue, which she carefully folded into a square.

"Is that a present?" Dottie appeared out of nowhere, and Mo quickly slipped the dark blue square into her pocket. "Who's it for?"

"That's for me to know and you to never find out as long as you live."

Dottie slid her thumb sideways into her mouth,

something she did only when she was really tired, or confused, or hurt. What a long day this had been!

"Ashley never got out of the compost. She's dead and gone." Dottie chewed her thumb. "Why'd she do that?" She looked at Mo as if Mo would have an answer.

"She . . . she couldn't help it."

"That's no excuse." It was what Mo always told her, when Dottie claimed she couldn't help eating cookies before dinner, or running through the Baggotts' sprinkler with her good shoes on. "Right?"

"Hey, come on," Mo answered. "Let's go get Daddy."

At the corner, a passing bus belched a black cloud. Dottie slipped her hand into Mo's without being told. They crossed the street and walked past the Tip Top Club, which breathed its sweet smoky breath out onto the sidewalk, past Abdul's Market, where the sidewalk was peppered with scratched-off lottery tickets, past the drawn pink curtains of Madame Rosa's Fortunes Told Closed for Vacation, past the empty lot where they'd once found a dead dog, which still made Dottie hum loudly every time they passed it, all the way to the middle school, where practice was winding down. Mo and Dottie climbed up in the bleachers just as Mr. Wren stepped up to the plate. When Dottie shouted, he swept off his cap and bowed to them, then gave their private signal—two fingers touching his brow, then pointing to right field. That meant this hit was just for them.

Whack.

"Yaaaay, Daddy!" screamed the Wild Child. "You the man!"

He hit another, and another, the ball arcing straight and true from the edge of his bat. His teammates high-fived him, and grinning, he clapped them on the back.

Look how happy he was. From head to toe. One big human happiness. A completely different person from the angry man in the water department uniform or the nervous man in the knotted tie.

Sitting in the bleachers, Mo imagined him happy all the time. Behind the bar of the Home Plate, serving cheesy omelets and juicy burgers and ice-cold beer, joking and talking with the customers. His own naturally happy self. The way he was meant to be. The way he'd been, before.

When happiness was his domain.

All day long Mo had struggled to think, and not succeeded, but now her thoughts tugged her down a dark road, leading her somewhere she didn't want to go. Her father would never be happy if things went on the way they were. His dream would wither and wilt like all of Fox Street's unwatered gardens and grass, all the lovely green life gone out of them.

What'd I tell you about thinking too much? You're going to get yourself in big trouble one of these days.

She slid her hand into her pocket and closed her fingers around the square of dark blue paper.

To leave their house and move away would be to abandon everything, everything she knew and loved, everything that made her feel safe. Not just feel, that measly word. *Made* her safe. Made her Mo.

To go would mean leaving behind her fox. That, most of all. Just when Mo was getting closer, when what she'd longed and waited for so patiently had given her a true sign. How could Mo abandon her?

It was unthinkable, even for a thinker.

"Who's that present for?"

Mo hadn't realized she was clutching the packet of fur in her pocket, but Dottie had. Her X-ray vision penetrated Mo's shorts.

"Me? Huh? Me, right?"

"Mind your own business," Mo told her, in a tone so harsh that, miracle of miracles, Dottie grew quiet.

Another Gift, If That Was
What You Wanted to Call It

"So. The facts as we know them. B and B want Fox Street, and they're willing to do whatever it takes to get it. They're targeting your dad." Mercedes tapped her chin. "My guess is they're counting on the domino effect. Meaning, one falls and all the others can't help but follow. If he sells . . ."

"Which will never happen," Mo said automatically.

The two of them hunkered on the floor of Da's porch, out of Starchbutt's sight. They'd swept it clean of winter dirt, but still you had to arrange yourself carefully in order to avoid splinters in certain tender body parts. What Mo really needed now was a refreshing glass of Da's extra-tart lemonade—just the thought of it made her pucker up. But Da was inside, napping on the couch.

Mercedes peeled off a sliver of wood and regarded it. She cocked her head in that familiar, quizzical, hungry-bird way. "Let's just say, for the sake of argument, that your dad gets struck by lightning, and when he comes to, he begins speaking in Japanese, and when we find a translator, she explains how your dad is saying he wants to sell the house to Buckman."

"Ha! So funny I forgot to laugh. Never. He'll never—"

"Mo! We have to examine all the possibilities!"

"Okay, okay, but even if he did." Mo swallowed. She gently pushed a ladybug corpse through a crack in the porch floor, down into the cemetery below. "There wouldn't be a domino effect. Because Mrs. Petrone wouldn't sell out. Mrs. Steinbott wouldn't, unless he pays in solid gold. And . . ." Mo paused for emphasis. "For sure, Da wouldn't."

She waited for Mercedes to agree. Seconds ticked by. More seconds.

"We're talking *Da*!" Mo said at last. "Who's lived

on Fox Street even longer than me! Who had to face discrimination and all kinds of bad juju to buy her house! Da, who stands taller on six toes than most people do on ten!" Mo shouted these last words, causing the sparrows to burst out of the old lilac with indignant peeps.

As if Mo's words gave off a bad smell, Mercedes wrinkled her fine-tuned nose. But before either could say anything more, her phone rang. She wiggled it out of her jeans pocket.

"Cornelius! Just what I need."

"Don't answer."

"He'll just leave a pompous, boring message. It's easier to answer and try to annoy him." Mercedes pressed the phone. "Wazzup, dawg?"

She stood up but immediately wheeled about and fled inside. Peeking around the porch railing, Mo beheld Mrs. Steinbott at the bottom of the porch steps.

"You!" Her voice was loud and accusing.

"Yup. It's me again." Mo lumbered to her feet. How in the world had she gotten into this go-between role? Stationed on the crumbly front walk, Mrs. Steinbott wore a black suit that stunk of mothballs. On her feet were black shoes so tiny, Cinderella might have trouble wedging her feet in. She looked headed for a funeral, except that she was . . . wait.

Was Mrs. Steinbott smiling? One corner of her mouth had gone up but not the other side, as if the mechanism were rusted.

"Wow," Mo said. "You're . . . you're all dressed up. You look very, very . . ."

"The time has come. Where did she go?"

"She had an important phone call."

Mrs. Steinbott clutched a handbag the size of a microwave. An uncertain look stole into her eyes. In spite of herself, Mo added, "But she said to be sure and tell you hi."

Just then a stampede of Baggotts pounded down the street. Armed with Super Soakers and dirt bombs, they went into slo-mo at the sight of Starchbutt. An evil grin spread across the face of Leo, possessor of the reattached finger. He raised his gun to his shoulder and took aim.

"Wicked witch alert!" he yelled to his brothers. "Prepare to fire!"

Mo ran down the steps and leaped into the space between the Baggotts and Mrs. Steinbott. "Just try it!" she yelled. "I'll tell my father you've been playing with the hose all week, and your mother will get slapped with a fine so fast you guys won't see daylight for weeks!"

Mo knew this wasn't true—the Baggotts never got punished for anything—but it sounded good. The other Baggotts threw their hands into the air. Leo Baggott sneered but slowly lowered the gun.

"Mo Wren and the witch. Nya nya nya-nya nya. Takes one to know one!"

One definitely lame dirt bomb landed at Mo's feet, and the boys reverse-stampeded up the street.

"Don't worry." Mo cocked her thumb toward the Baggott dust cloud. "I'll get their big brother to read them the riot act."

To Mo's bewilderment, Mrs. Steinbott's brittle edges all seemed to soften. "Boys will be boys," she said. "My own could get up to some mischief, especially when he was around *her*."

Mo's own heart turned over.

"I'm . . . I'm sorry about your son, Mrs. Steinbott."

The knuckles gripping the monstrous purse went white.

"By now he'd be a grown man." Her face was like a piece of paper somebody'd balled up in their fist, then felt bad about and tried to smooth back out. "Ten years older than the last time I saw him."

A lump rose in Mo's throat. "Think of that."

"Oh, I do. I do, every day."

"I'm sorry," Mo said again.

She lifted her hand, almost as if she meant to give Mo a pat, but then thought better of it. Instead she reached into the big purse and tugged out . . . another purse, nearly as big. For a moment Mo feared she'd open that and pull out another one, and then another one, like something in a nightmare.

Instead Starchbutt pushed it toward Mo. Her face was full of urgency.

"This could be the last summer," she said.

Dread got Mo in its clutches. "What are you talking about?"

"What if I hadn't opened it? Something made me open it."

The poor thing really is demented, Mo told herself. Just be nice to her. Don't get her any more upset.

"She has to have this!" She pushed the purse into Mo's hands. "Right away."

"Okay."

"You promise me."

"I promise."

Mrs. Steinbott continued to stand there, her mothball smell rising in the heat. Mo was afraid that she meant to wait till Mercedes finally came back out, but at last, as if she'd convinced herself she could trust

Mo after all, she turned around. On the edge of the curb, she wavered. Mo rushed forward and caught her arm. Mrs. Steinbott stared across the street as if she'd lost track of where she was.

"Do you know how long it's been since I crossed this street?" she asked Mo.

"Long."

"Longer than the Mississippi." She smiled again and this time managed to get both corners of her mouth in sync. "Headed my way?" She crooked her arm.

Arm in arm, each carrying a big purse, they looked both ways, then stepped out into Fox Street.

Demolition

CORNELIUS CHRISTIAN CUNNINGHAM had somehow gotten the idea that the only way to truly ascertain the facts of Da's situation was to see it with his own eyes. Somehow he found Mercedes's detailed reports vague. Confounding and confusing. Not to mention puzzling and perplexing. Possibly phony and fake.

"The man can't keep his big ugly nose out of our business!" Mercedes complained.

"Child, he's married to your mother now. You and I *are* his business, like it or not."

Da was on the couch again, a blank crossword on her lap. They made the puzzles too easy these days, she complained. Not enough of a challenge. She shifted, rearranging her legs, which, thank heavens, ended in a pair of closed-toe sandals. Da clenched her jaw.

"You okay?" Mo asked her.

"These poor old feet of mine itch up a tempest every night. And then just as I drift off to sleep, toe pain will shoot through me and startle me awake." Da put a hand to her brow. "It's always in a toe that's not really there. Phantom pain, the doctors call it." She let her crossword puzzle slip from her fingers. "Give me strength, I'm a walking haunted house."

"How about some tea?"

"Tea's for sick folk." She ran her tongue over her lips and sighed. "Just a small cup. What would I do without you two? My crown is in my heart, not on my head."

Mercedes and Mo slipped into the kitchen.

"I'm seriously worried," Mercedes said, filling the kettle. "If Corny sees Da lying on the couch, muttering she's haunted . . ." She gave the faucet handle a shove, but it kept on dripping. "Not to mention how much work this house needs." She banged the kettle onto the stove. "Not to mention, did you notice Da's not exactly protesting his meddling?"

Mo pressed her fingers to her temples.

"I'm having trouble thinking straight these days," she said. "I—"

A commotion outside the front door cut off any possibility of thought whatsoever.

"Mo! Mercey!" Dottie shrieked. "Help! Save it!"

Mo ran outside. A crowd was gathered at the end of the street, where a yellow machine with thick rubber treads occupied the front lawn of the A.O.L. House. Its steel arm dangled an enormous, menacing claw over the roof.

"What's going on?" Mo demanded.

Mr. Duong, the fix-it man, polished his glasses on the hem of his shirt. "My guess is they're not here to landscape the place, Mo," he said. At that moment, the claw rumbled to life. "Uh-oh."

Crash. The closed claw punched into the mossy little roof, caving it with one blow. Shingles flew, wooden boards splintered. Who knew a roof was so flimsy? The claw reared up, landed another blow, and there were the house's innards, *splat*, on display for all to see. Strips of bent metal, dangling wires. That was how fast things could change. With a whoop, Gem Baggott hurled a rock at the front door. Mrs. Petrone grabbed him by the neck of his T-shirt.

"Don't you dare!" she scolded. "Show some respect!"

"It's just a beat-up old rathole anyway!" he protested, wiggling free.

The claw punched the house again. Mo had to cover her eyes. It was as if they were watching a bully beat a helpless person to a pulp, and there was nothing anyone could do to stop it.

"Someone has plans for this property," Mr. Duong told Mrs. Petrone. He crossed his arms and rocked back on his heels. "We are witnessing capitalism at work."

Mrs. Petrone scratched her head, which today was styled into curls that stuck to her cheeks like uppercase Gs.

"I get a very bad feeling about it, whatever it is," she said.

Now Mercedes came rushing up, followed by Mrs. Baggott, her flip-flops going *flop* but not *flip*. Mr. and Mrs. Hernandez, who owned Tortilla Feliz, showed up, their hands covered with flour, and Ms. Hugg ran as fast as her tight red dress allowed. Before long, someone from every house but Mrs. Steinbott's and the Kowalski house was watching.

"I wish Daddy was here," Dottie said. "He'd make them stop, right? He'd stop those doo-doo heads, right?" She slid her thumb into her mouth, popped it back out. "Right, Mo?"

122

"Buckman." Venom dripped from Mercedes's voice. "He means business, all right."

A dump truck backed down the street, inching between the parked cars. Its rear fender collided with the guardrail, adding yet another dent. The driver jumped down, scowling.

"Mister!" Mrs. Petrone waved him over.

The driver took off his yellow hard hat, as if out of respect for the crowd. He had a ponytail and kindly eyes.

"Sorry about your guardrail. Backing a rig in here is like threading a needle with a . . ." He scratched his head, searching for a good comparison. "A . . . a . . ."

"Never mind!" Mrs. Petrone waved a hand. "What we want to know is what's going on here? What do you know about all this?"

"A hippo, maybe," the driver said.

"You're funny," Dottie told him. She helped herself to his hat and settled it on her head.

"We're demoing to the ground," he explained. "Everything's slated for teardown, that's what I hear."

A silence fell. They all stared at him. He scratched his head some more and nudged a rock with his boot toe.

"I hear office park."

They continued to stare.

"Maybe a little light industry? But all green, you

know. All nice and up-to-the-minute." He tapped Dottie's hard-hatted head. "Anybody home?"

"You been clobbered by a two-by-four, young man?" demanded Mrs. Petrone.

"Not that I know of." He retrieved his hard hat. "You all have a nice day now."

As he retreated to the truck, Mo chased after him.

"Does the name Buckman sound familiar?"

The driver swung up into his cab. He rubbed the space between his kindly eyes. "I'm not very good at names." He smiled down at her. "Don't you worry your pretty little head, missy. These are grown-up matters! Whatever happens, your mama will take good care of you!" He shifted the truck's gears and backed toward the growing pile of rubble.

Mr. Duong pushed his glasses back up his nose. Ms. Hugg murmured some inappropriate language. Mrs. Baggott ground out her cigarette with her flip-flop. Mr. and Mrs. Hernandez clasped each other's hands. Mrs. Petrone voiced the question in everyone's head.

"How come we haven't heard a single word about this?" Her pillowy chest rose and fell. "Some big kahunas are after our property. Big-time! How can they have kept this a secret from every last one of us?" She looked from face to face and settled on Mr. Duong. Her eyes narrowed. "What was that you said about capitalism?"

Mr. Duong looked alarmed. "I was speculating, that's all. I don't know any more than any of you."

"I wouldn't be surprised if Mrs. Steinbott had her finger in this." Mrs. Baggott flicked a bit of tobacco from her tongue. "She's rich. And the rich only get richer."

Mrs. Petrone peered at Mo. "*Bella,* you look like you saw a ghost. You don't know anything about this, do you?"

Everyone stared at Mo the way they'd stared at the truck driver. The knowledge of her father's two letters, and the meeting he'd had with B and B, surged up inside her and tried to blurt itself out. He thinks you're dominoes! she wanted to say. If we don't band together, he'll knock us all down!

But they'd demand to know where she got that information, and she'd have to tell them her father was already dealing with Buckman. And how could she betray her father?

Mercedes clamped her lips together, as if she, too, had words trying to jump out of her mouth. But she didn't speak. Instead she waited, watching Mo.

"How . . . how would I know about it?" Mo heard herself say.

And One More Gift

WITHIN DAYS THE A.O.L. HOUSE had vanished. *Poof!* The ground was so dry, the machines hadn't even left any tracks. All that remained was a caution-taped pile of dirt, which the Baggotts immediately commandeered for a fort.

Mo squinted at the spot where the house had stood, almost seeing it, the way when the moon's a crescent, you can still perceive the whole. She picked a bouquet of daisies and laid it where the front door once stood.

But what she couldn't do, no matter how fiercely she tried, was think two thoughts in a row.

Single solitary thoughts Mo was capable of:

126

1. He's a good dad. Unlike Mercedes's real dad, whoever that is. Not to mention her bonehead stepdad.
2. If you allow there's such a thing as necessary evil, and it seems as if most people do, where do you draw the line? Does that include necessary stealing? Necessary lying and cheating? Necessary betraying your neighbors on the street where you've lived all your life and everyone has watched out for you, not to mention your little sister?
3. Even though people have seen skunks and raccoons and even hawks, no one on Fox Street has seen a fox. Those other animals hardly even seem wild anymore. But my fox is different. My shy, beautiful fox.
4. One of the rocks I found that day was shaped exactly like a heart.

But no matter how Mo tried to link these thoughts together, they stayed separate, rolling around her mind like the beads of a broken necklace. She could not coax them onto a string.

Back up the street, Pi was busy waxing a curb with the end of a fat candle. How did he always manage to be around when she was feeling lonesome?

"Hey." He stood up. An angry red scrape just above his cheekbone made her wince. He touched his fingers to it and shrugged.

"Road rash."

"You ought to be more careful."

A smile bloomed in his beat-up face. He shrugged. "The way I figure it is, if you don't fall, you're not trying hard enough."

"That's stupid," Mo said.

Pi's smile slid off into the dirt. Right away she wished she could take it back. What was stupid about trying hard, about taking a risk, about wishing to fly? Everything, that's what! It was worse than stupid to gamble with gravity. Stay put, stay on the ground, stay safe!

Pi turned away, resuming his waxing.

"Strange," he said to the curb. "Some people think they know everything."

Not me! Just turn around and I'll tell you how tangled up my brain is!

But Pi kept his back to her, and on she trudged.

Mrs. Petrone was stepping out her front door, wearing her black pantsuit, which meant she was headed for the funeral home. When Mo waved, she merely nodded and hurried down the driveway to climb into the hearse. Mr. Duong, sitting on his porch reading a repair manual, didn't seem to hear her when she called hello. This was how it had been on the street, ever since they flattened the A.O.L. House. Suspicion and distrust wheeled over the street like a flock of pigeons, settling first on this house, then on that one.

The little tissue-paper square that she carried in her pocket at all times had begun to fray, so now she kept it inside a Ziploc bag. Yesterday she'd hauled a jug down to the stream, which had dried up even more, and poured water out into a couple of pie pans. If the foxes couldn't find enough to drink, they'd be forced out into the open. They'd have to make their way closer to the park's picnic areas, against all their instincts. Mo couldn't bear to think of the fox mother leading her kits into possible danger. What if they were crossing the parking lot in the dark, and some car came swerving out of nowhere, and . . .

She closed her fingers tight around the little bag. Forget the ban. She'd bring more water down there this afternoon. And every afternoon until it finally rained. If it ever rained again. Of course it would rain again. Things had to get better. Unless they didn't.

But they had to. Mo drew the Ziploc bag out of her pocket.

"Lemme see!" Dottie materialized, waving her sticky hands. The one treasure Mo owned, the one and only thing she tried to keep private and hers alone, and Dottie was after it night and day. Not that she had any idea that fox fur was what the little parcel contained. Not that Mo would ever share it with her, or anyone. "Just once lemme see lemme see lemme see lemme—"

"How many times do I have to tell you?" Mo pushed her, harder than she meant to. "This. Is. Not. For. You!"

"Queen of Mean!"

And Dottie was the Princess of Mess. Only far, far worse than usual. The snarls in her hair had become permanent—nothing but scissors would cure them. And that T-shirt—when was the last time she'd changed it? So extensive was her grubbiness, she appeared to be wearing dirt-colored pads on her knees and elbows. Mo had been neglecting things, all right. The realization made her even angrier.

"I've got enough to worry about!" Mo jammed the bag back into her pocket. "I'm sick of always looking out for you. Sick and tired, you hear me? Go away. Vanish."

Dottie pulled her thumb out of her mouth. She was sucking her thumb all the time now. "You're a boa conflicter!"

In disgust, Mo turned her back and stomped away, back up the street toward home. A leech! A sucker-fish, forever glued to Mo's side! Mo stomped past Mrs. Steinbott, who was sitting on her porch, of course. All Mo needed now was for her to yell "You!" and deliver another one of her wacko witch prophecies. The sky is falling! The end is near! The big ugly purse was still under Mo's bed, where she'd tossed it along with the jar of bubble bath, rather than upset Mercedes with another so-called present. Sure enough, Mrs. Steinbott leaned over her porch railing.

"The little dickens!" She jabbed her knitting needle in the direction of the Wrens' front yard.

Someone had meticulously arranged a row of beer bottles along the walk. That someone had filled each bottle with water and set inside each a daisy or buttercup from the Green Kingdom.

Except, that is, for the two bottles at the very foot of the front steps. Each of them held a furled yellow rosebud. One kiss of the sun and those velvet petals would open, sharing the secret wrapped inside.

Who but the Wild Child could dream up a beer-bottle garden? Mo sat on the top front step and gazed out over it. The sun that refused to stop shining tapped the bottles with its dazzling wand, turning them emerald and diamond and smoky topaz.

Mrs. Steinbott's weaselly eyes saw everything. She had to know Dottie had plundered her roses. Had she already called the police? Or was she saving up her wrath for when Mr. Wren came home? Or would she nab Dottie herself and scare the living you-know-what out of her?

Or did she find the garden as beautiful as Mo did?

The daisies and buttercups nodded in the breeze, like skinny-necked old ladies listening to dance music.

What if necessary evil had an opposite? This is what it would be. This unnecessary good.

For the first time in days, Mo smiled.

Home Plate

DOTTIE SAT BESIDE DA at the Walcott kitchen table, inching word by word through a picture book.

"The woods were dark," she intoned. "A cold wind made her shrink."

"Shiver," said Da.

"At last she saw a house. Oh, God, she told herself."

"Oh, *good*," whispered Mo.

"I can take shhh . . . shepherds here."

"*Shelter*," said Da. "You've got the 'sh' sound down solid, Dorothea Wren. Kiss your brain."

Dottie smooched her fingers, then smacked herself in the forehead.

Footsteps sounded in the hall. Mr. Wren, freshly showered and wearing his favorite Wahoo T-shirt, poked his head through the kitchen doorframe.

"Daddy! You're home?"

Mr. Wren grinned. "I had to leave early—important business," he said. "Da, would it be all right if the Little Bit hangs with you for a while? I need to borrow my partner, Mo."

"It's far more than all right." Da lifted her chin the Walcott way. "This is my star pupil."

"Where we going, Daddy?" Mo asked as they climbed into the car.

"I've got something to show just you."

They cruised up Paradise and onto the highway. Lake Erie was flat and blue, like a distant mirage. Mr. Wren sang along with the radio, his voice extra loud because the car's air-conditioning had conked out and both their windows were rolled all the way down. His voice trilled up high as a girl's, then dropped down into his shoes.

Mo remembered sitting in the backseat as her parents sang duets. One of their favorites was "I Got You Babe." Every time they sang that line, they'd both point over the seat, at her.

Today empty warehouses and factories flew by, a

134

blur as she squinted into the wind. Where were they going? Oh, Mo hated surprises. But her father's happiness was contagious. It was like the wind itself, catching you up, carrying you along with it.

When a song she liked came on, Mo began to sing, too. Her father tried to harmonize, their voices twining together like the strands of a sturdy rope. Mo began to wish they'd never get wherever they were headed, that they'd just ride around and around like this, happy together, the car a little houseboat floating on the summer afternoon, till at last the sun dropped into the lake and they'd sail back toward Fox Street.

But Mr. Wren took an exit, passing a hospital and a bunch of apartment buildings and easing into a neighborhood of old-fashioned houses that had seen better days. The ground floors had been turned into shops. They passed a bookstore, a bakery, a café, a place selling homemade ice cream. Some had colorful awnings and little tables set out on the sidewalk. Flowers bloomed in boxes and tubs. The upstairs windows were hung with curtains or shades. A white cat solemnly stared down as they went by.

Mr. Wren pulled up in front of a dark green house with curlicue trim over the windows and along the edge of the roof. The bottom floor was built out and fitted with a big plate-glass window. CORKY'S TAVERN said the faded sign over the door. FOR LEASE OR SALE read the sign in the window.

Cupping their hands around their eyes, they pressed their noses to the window. A small bar with stools ran across the back wall. There was space for tables, and the corners were snug with wooden booths. Dingy linoleum covered the floor.

"It needs some TLC, that's for sure," said Mr. Wren. "But wait'll you see the upstairs. Three nice little bedrooms, one with built-in shelves ready-made for Dot's bottles."

Mo stepped back from the window. "You already saw the upstairs?"

Mr. Wren took her hand. "Come on, come see the backyard."

A crooked white fence covered with blooming vines looped around its edges. The yard was empty, not a single tree, the sun pouring down.

"I was thinking that'd be the perfect spot for a little vegetable garden. We could grow our own tomatoes and herbs for the sandwiches and soups."

Mr. Wren gently lobbed his invisible baseball into the invisible garden.

"It's a good neighborhood, Momo. I met a guy who runs his own hardware store, and a gal who's looking to open a teahouse. It's just like Fox Street, except things are looking up instead of down. There's hope in the air." He scooped the air. "See it?"

He drew her to the back kitchen window and pointed out the nice new grill, the fryers where the best onion rings in town would sizzle. The cooler would hold all kinds of beer, but chocolate milk and all-natural fruit juice, too, because this was going to be a family place, where everybody in the neighborhood felt at home.

"Corky, the old owner, fell on hard times. But that just means a better price."

The excitement in her father's voice worked a spell, and in spite of herself, Mo saw the two of them, side by side, sweeping and scrubbing and painting. She saw herself doing her homework in one of the corner booths, and heard her father's laughter from behind the bar as he sliced a home-grown tomato for a delicious BLT. Mo glanced up at the curlicued windows. She could see the small face with a lollipop jutting out, waving down at her.

"You know the best part?" he asked her.

"What?"

"I'd never have to leave the two of you again." His voice went crooked. "We'd be together all the time. I . . . I could quit asking too much of you, Locomo."

"You don't!"

"Yeah, I do." Suddenly he sounded angry. "It hasn't been fair, no way. I want us to be more of a family again. We could be . . . we could almost be like we used to be."

A red bird flashed across the yard, looking for a tree to perch in. Mo felt its shadow flutter in her chest. What kind of yard had no place for a bird to nest, no place for a girl to settle her spine and think? Frightened, Mo dug her hand into her pocket. Where was it? Had it fallen out somewhere? Frantic, she shoved her fingers into her other pocket and there, there it was.

"Got an itch?" asked her father.

Words beat inside her, like a bird trapped inside a house, and she longed to tell him. But what if he didn't understand? Her father was different from her. He'd tell her, "You've never seen a fox, Momo. You can't abandon something you're not sure exists."

"I am sure," she said aloud.

Mr. Wren gave her a funny look. His curls made a dark halo around his head, and his eyes shone so bright, Mo realized with a little shock that they were full of tears.

"There are a lot of things we haven't talked about, aren't there? That's my fault, too. I've been a coward."

"Daddy . . ."

"Don't go making excuses for me. I won't have you doing that anymore." He put a finger to her lips. "Listen to me now. When . . . when your mom was still alive, she made me so happy, she filled up my life with so much light and sweetness—back then, I could work any job, handle any kind of junk, just so long as I had her to come home to. But ever since . . . since . . ."

The red bird, a cardinal, was uncertain as a spark, flitting from fence to ground and back again.

"Life's not going to wait for you. If there's one thing losing her taught me, that's it. The world just keeps barreling forward, ready or not." He slipped an arm around her. "I need to start over, Mo. I've got to take hold of things. I need to leave the bad things behind and make something new for all of us."

Her father never talked like this. A small door, a door she hadn't even known was there, not to mention shut, creaked open inside her.

"I lay awake a lot of nights, and you know what? I'm convinced she'd think it was the right thing to do.

She couldn't stand any of us hurting. Any time you cried, she'd cry too. I remember when you got your first haircut, she—"

"No!" Mo buried her face against his chest. The door swung wider, letting in a hot rush of pain. "Please, Daddy. I don't want to move. It's too far away. We don't know anybody here! Who'd cut my hair? Who'd tutor Dottie? What about the Den? What about Starchbutt?"

Mr. Wren laughed. "Whaaa?"

"Daddy, I'd miss Mercedes too much!"

"It seems far, but it's really just ten miles. I'd drive over and pick her up anytime you wanted. I promise." He lifted her chin. "You trust me, don't you?"

Looking away, Mo watched the cardinal settle on an overhead wire.

"I've finally got the perfect name for our place," Mr. Wren said softly. "I can't believe we didn't think of it before. You ready?"

She shook her head.

"The Wren House. Get it? We'll decorate with birdhouses and feature one on our sign."

"That's stupid!" The door inside her slammed shut. *Bam.* "We already have a Wren house!"

Mr. Wren let her go. The lines between his eyes, the

trunk of the tree that arched up and disappeared in the shadows of his baseball cap—those lines seemed to grow deeper, harsher, even as she looked. All the joy drained out of him now. He cast his eyes down as if he could see it on the ground, a puddle of lost happiness.

"Too bad," he said. The cardinal began to sing, its silvery song tumbling all around them. "I was hoping you'd be more open-minded. Maybe even glad."

"That Buckman's a creep!" Mo cried. "He wants to knock our house down!"

Mr. Wren's face darkened. "A house is just four walls and a roof. You can put a price on a house the same as a car or a baseball team or a pedigree poodle. And when that price all of a sudden skyrockets, you'd be a fool not—"

"How come you're the only one on the street who knows what Buckman's doing?"

"There's such a thing as asking too many questions." He was scowling now. "You know when a chance like this is going to come our way again? Never, that's when. 'I hit big or I miss big.' Babe Ruth, not Shakespeare, but it works for me."

A single forgotten beer bottle lay near the building's foundation. Mr. Wren nudged it with the toe of his sneaker. "Believe me, Mo. I wish I could tell you life was always fair."

"You want to buy this place and so you'll do anything! You'll make a sleazy deal. You'll betray everyone else. You'll ruin my life. You don't care!"

The cardinal broke off its song midnote, and the bird arrowed out of sight. The yard grew cemetery quiet.

"This conversation's over." Mr. Wren pulled his cap low over his face. "I'm the one making this decision. Your job's to get used to it." With that, he strode toward their car.

Mo grabbed the beer bottle and hurled it at the side of the house. The sound of it smashing zapped her like an electric shock. *Yes!* Whole one second and destroyed the next. Just like that. The blink of an eye.

"No!" she shouted. "I don't trust you! And I never will again, as long as I live!"

Wild currents shot through her. At her feet glittered bits and pieces no one could ever put back together.

Traitor, Part 2

IT WAS A CHALLENGE, living in a house as small as the Wrens' and refusing to speak to someone else who lived there, but Mo was determined. For the next three days, she wouldn't even meet her father's eyes, much less answer his questions or acknowledge his lame jokes. If she absolutely had to communicate with him, she put it in writing.

Messages and replies written in fury:

I think Dottie has another cavity.

Your uniform is in the dryer.

The TV is broken again.

No.

No.

No.

No.

Meanwhile, Mercedes's father troubles were thickening, too.

"It's like a surprise attack! Except he warned us!" Her eyes were wide. "He's coming! Tomorrow!"

"She's the one who should come."

Mercedes drew a deep breath. Her next words fell one by one, like medicine from a dropper. "She is. She's coming."

"Your mom's coming to Fox Street?"

Here it was, something Mo and Merce had wished for so many years: Monette coming home. Only now, it was far from the happy occasion they'd always dreamed about. Now it was a water-main break. A summer-long drought. A disaster.

"She says she has something to tell me." Mercedes's

144

golden eyes were wide. "Something big."

Mo grabbed a broom. "We've got twenty-four hours to get this house looking beautiful."

She took the kitchen, which was in the worst shape, while Mercedes started in on the dining room. Someone from church had taken Da grocery shopping, so she couldn't protest or get insulted as they scoured her house. Mo pulled the vegetable drawer out of the refrigerator and filled it with hot, soapy water.

"We'll show him," she reassured Mercedes, who was dusting the dining room. "We'll whip the place into shape, and he'll see it's perfectly fine for Da to stay here."

A rainbow-kissed bubble drifted up from the sink. Watching it rise made Mo feel strangely off balance, as if one leg had grown shorter than the other. All at once she saw herself in the kitchen of Corky's Tavern, loading the dishwasher, Dad flipping an omelet, the two of them attempting harmony—*pop!* The bubble broke. Mo blinked.

"What did you say?" called Mercedes from the other room.

"All Da needs is someone to come in and clean once in a while." Taking a deep breath, she recommenced scrubbing with all her might. "And I bet her church would help with meals if she let them. Don't you think?"

Mercedes appeared in the kitchen doorway, dust rag in hand. Her nose wrinkled and her eyes shut and she pulled her head back against her neck as if someone were trying to kiss her, but the sneeze changed its mind.

"I can't . . ."

The sneeze changed its mind again.

"Aa . . . aa . . . aaaa!"

Mercedes collapsed into a sneezing fit. She yanked open the door and flung the dusty cloth out. "This is bonkerdom! I'm allergic to this whole house. Aaaa-*choo!*"

Another soap bubble rose in the sunlight. Mo wheeled away from the sink. "Come on, rock paper scissors—loser gets the bathroom."

In reply, Mercedes draped her lengthy self over a chair. She looked worn out, though they'd barely gotten started.

"We have a stellar cleaning lady. Monette and Corny and me."

"For real?"

"She cleans my room. I never have to do anything except put my clothes in the wash."

"Wow." Mo peeled away her sticky T-shirt and blew down her sweaty front. "I could get used to that."

Mercedes sat up, looking encouraged. "You know what I'm thinking? Next summer you'll come stay with *me*. I've got an extra bed in my room, just for sleepovers. With a lame pink princess canopy, but still. I'll take you to a park you'll love. It's colossal, acres and acres, with a pond and cool little paddle-boats."

"Wow. It sounds like a plan. I visit down there for a few days, then we come up here for the rest of the summer. I like it!"

Mercedes leaned back, legs and arms flopping as if she'd been deboned.

"Did I mention the juicer? Three-C makes these concoctions from fresh mango and pineapple, and I have to admit they're almost supernatural. Oh, yeah, and the TV's down in the family room, about half a mile from their bedroom. We can stay up all night, no problem."

"Wow," said Mo, stuck on REPLAY. "You make it sound like paradise. I mean, real paradise, not Paradise Avenue."

"It's different from here, Mo."

"Rock scissors paper." Mo tucked her fingers

behind her back. "We don't want His Royal Pain in the Butt to have a nervous breakdown when he sees this place."

Mercedes's spine melted. "Mo, I've got something to say."

"Okay."

"We've been friends for all of our formative years. We are sisters in some parallel universe. No one else knows that I used to be terrified of bridges."

"You still are."

"See? And I know you secretly like Pi Baggott, even though you'd never admit it even to me."

"I need someone for a friend when you're not around." Mo's cheeks grew toasty. "That's all."

"So that's why I'm going to tell you this. I've been trying to tell you all summer, but you haven't exactly been receptive."

Mo braced herself against the sink. It was so quiet in the kitchen, she could hear the soap bubbles popping one by one.

"Suppose—" Mercedes poked her finger at her bottom lip. "Suppose the planet stops spinning, and Da's brain gets taken over by aliens, or more likely by my mother and stepfather. Suppose she agrees to move downstate with us—wait! Don't say anything yet! Let me finish."

Pop pop pop. It was amazing, how deafening the sound of a bubble popping could be.

"That might not be the complete and utter disaster you think." Mercedes began to lift her chin, but an invisible weight tugged it back down. "Because . . . because I might really need her. As my ally. In case. They decide to, you know. Procreate."

Mo was stunned. Never once in all her extensive thinking had she considered this possibility.

"They haven't said it, not in actual words! But a blind man could see. They're in love, Mo! They dance in the kitchen. They kiss any time, any place. She'll be sitting at the computer and he—"

"Okay, okay, I get the idea."

"It's just a matter of time! That might even be what Monette's coming here to tell me. Oh, they'll pretend I'm part of the big decision, but it won't really matter what I say or feel. Irrationality's going to win out. And then?" Mercedes flung her hands over her eyes. "Life as I know it will come to an end."

"You might be exaggerating. Being a big sister isn't all that bad."

Mercedes lowered her hands and stared. "I've witnessed with my own eyes what you go through. The torture, the unrelenting hardship! Dottie gets away with everything, while you're expected to be responsible and mature no matter what. Fairness is a meaningless word, once you have a little brother or sister. Not to mention you have to share, and I hate to share."

Mercedes's arms and legs wove themselves into a knot. She pressed her forehead to her knee. When she spoke again, it was to the very center of her golden self.

"Not to mention. It'll have a father."

Mo racked her brain but could think of no way to deny that.

"That won't be fair," Mercedes said. "Right from the start, things won't be fair."

Mo turned back to the sink, where the water had gone cold and murky and every last bubble had popped.

"If I had Da living with me, it'd be different. Da's *mine*, you know? And we'd be together, twenty-four seven. We wouldn't have to be separated half the year, the way we are now. Families are supposed to stick together—let me see, what famous person said that? Shakespeare?" Mercedes raised her head. She cocked it in that infuriating way of hers. "Oh, wait, I know: Maureen Jewel Wren!"

Mo ran a finger around the vegetable drawer, so clean now it squeaked. She dried it with a towel, then slid it back inside the refrigerator.

"Why aren't you saying anything?" Mercedes demanded.

"What can I say? You already have it all figured out."

"You're mad at me." Mercedes undid her body knot and sat up very straight. "I knew you'd be mad."

"Please don't tell me what I am, thank you very much."

"I knew it," repeated Mo's once-best friend. "You can't stand things changing! You know what that makes you? It makes you a . . . a dictator! You want to be in charge of the whole world! Bossing every last person around, telling them how things are supposed to be, thank *you* very much. No one else's opinions or needs will be taken into account, sorry about that."

"Oh, yeah? That's what you think. You don't know everything about me, Mercedes Jasmine Walcott! Just because you wear better clothes than me and have a maid and all of a sudden you think Fox Street is the armpit of the world—"

"I never said that and you know it!"

"You've been faking all summer, pretending you were on my side!"

"I wasn't faking! I am on your side! It's . . . it's complicated, that's all. It's not black and white! Why can't you see that? What's the matter with you?"

"Me? I'm not the one who changed! I'm no traitor!"

"Consistency is the hobgoblin of small minds!"

"Who you calling a hobgoblin, you Benedict Arnold?"

A stricken look stole over Mercedes's face. Mo followed her gaze upward, along the length of her own arm, all the way to her hand, which clutched one of Da's good glasses. Which, it appeared, she was preparing to hurl across the room.

Mo lowered her arm. Even as she set the glass back on the counter, she could hear the sound it would make when it smashed. She could feel the thrilling, sickening electric jolt of it.

"I'm leaving," she said.

"Good idea."

"Better call your cleaning lady to finish up here."

Mercedes didn't say another word as Mo swept out the door.

That night she lay awake brooding, face toward her window. The sky shuddered with heat lightning. Even the sky was making false promises now. Heat lightning was nothing but bluster and brag, never delivering the sweet gift every blade of grass longed for, every dusty bird dreamed of.

At last, when all the lights in Da's house were out, Mo crept across the street and hooked the hideous purse on the doorknob. She'd considered throwing the thing in the trash, or down the ravine, but at the last minute she couldn't stand to betray old Starchbutt that way. But this was it. No more favors. No more running interference. From now on, Mercedes could fend for her own high-and-mighty self.

Standing there on that heaving sea of a front porch, Mo heard a faint rustle beneath her feet. A field mouse, probably. Yet for an instant it seemed as if all those bits of toys that had fallen through the porch cracks over the long years of friendship were stirring, coming to life just long enough to whisper *Good-bye.*

Creeping back home, she saw fireflies drifting up from the grass like the last sparks of a dying fire. She tiptoed into her room, locking the door behind her. Moments later, another creature of the night began to scratch at it.

"Mo! Mo, it's me!"

How could Mo have gone two whole years without

realizing all she had to do was lock her bedroom door? That was how simple it had been all along! *Click*. The turn of a lock, and she had her whole bed to herself. No leech taking up nine-tenths of the mattress. No suckerfish sucking the life out of her. How could Mo have been so stupid not to think of it before?

"Mo! Mo? Are you in there?"

Scritch, scratch, the little rat. Mo pulled the pillow over her ears, yet still she heard the sound, as if it came from inside her own head. Turning toward the window, she watched the jagged yellow streaks electrify Mrs. Steinbott's roses. A light burned upstairs, in the window just across from Mo's. Did that mental case stay up knitting all night long?

Or could it be that, all alone, she sometimes got scared of the dark?

The middle of the bed was so uncomfortable. Mo huddled on the edge, the way she usually did. One last feeble *scritch* and *scratch*, then silence.

A siren *whoop-whoop*ed up on Paradise. Mo kept her eyes on Mrs. Steinbott's light—the night-light of Fox Street—till at long last she fell asleep.

The Letter, Part 3

OPENING HER BEDROOM DOOR the next morning, she stepped into an ambush of tangled sheets and candy wrappers. Mo kicked them aside. Her eyes felt hot and grainy, as if she hadn't slept a single wink.

Downstairs, Dottie's cereal bowl, swimming with blue milk, sat on the floor in front of the TV. It was Saturday, and Dottie should have been deep into her lineup of favorite cartoons. Mr. Wren should have been trying to start the lawn mower, cursing, trying again, giving up, and borrowing Mr. Duong's.

Instead, ghost house.

At least he could have left a note. Just because she

wasn't speaking to him didn't mean he had no obligation to let her know where he was.

Unless he didn't want her to know where he was.

Mo rushed out the side door. The morning air smelled strangely burned, as if an angry giant had lit and blown out a forest's worth of matches. The sky hung low and heavy. On Mrs. Steinbott's clothesline, the boiled sponges should have been swaying in the kicking-up breeze, except her line was empty.

No sponges.

No cartoons.

No car.

No father.

She went back inside and did the dishes, but her hands were clumsy and she broke a glass. Cleaning up the pieces, she nicked her finger and stuck the Band-Aid on crooked, and later, when she put the laundry in, she dripped drops of blood on her father's T-shirt and had to rinse it in cold water and treat it with stain remover.

Wait'll I tell Mercedes.

Oh.

No best friend.

As the washer churned, Mo dragged herself up the basement steps. Her father had forgotten his cell phone, there on the counter. Mo looked out the front window. Da's front porch was empty. The handbag was gone from the knob. What time was Three-C due? Mo didn't know. The way things stood, she wouldn't even get to meet him. She'd be reduced to spying from across the street, just like Mrs. Steinbott.

Outside, the heat wrapped itself around her like a wool coat. The air smelled as if the sky were paper and the heat lightning had singed it all along the edges. Bag on his shoulder, Bernard the mailman strode up the sidewalk.

"Nothing but junk for the Wrens today. Sorry!" He handed Mo a bundle of circulars. "Instead it's other folks' turn to finally get their registered mail."

Mrs. Petrone stood on her lawn, refolding a sheet of paper, her lips pressed as straight as if they held a row of bobby pins. A few doors up, Mrs. Baggott paced her front porch, a sheet of paper in her hand, too. She was gabbing into her cell phone, her voice excited. Her shoes were actually going *flip* as well as *flop*.

Bernard knocked on Mrs. Steinbott's door. And knocked. Watching him shift the heavy bag on his shoulder, Mo's brain served up another one of Da's quotations. "Love is patient." She was sure there was more to it—love was gentle, maybe? Or was it strong? Or both? Her mind was fog. A cry cut through its swirling mist.

"Mo! Guess what?" The Wild Child tore across the street.

"Stop! Halt! What'd I tell you about looking both ways?"

Dottie jerked her head from side to side, though she was already on the sidewalk.

Mo grabbed her shoulder. "I thought you went with Daddy."

"Daddy?" Dottie wriggled free.

"The man who lives in our house? Where is he?"

But Dottie couldn't be bothered with boring questions.

"Guess what? The Baggotts got a letter. It's going to be M and M dough rain around here."

The back of Mo's neck prickled as if icy fingers had reached out and stroked it.

"Make sense," she hissed.

"M and M's!" Dottie giggled at her sister's stupidity. "I hope it's not peanut. I hope it's regular. And I hope the dough's quarters, not pennies."

Mrs. Steinbott cracked her door at last. Mo watched her take Bernard's pen and sign. The mailman clattered down the porch steps, climbed in his truck, and drove away.

"You're seriously grounded," Mo informed Dottie.

Dottie made a sound like a sick moose. "But it's going to rain candy! Candy and money!"

"Inside! Before I pulverize you!"

Dottie walked backward up the driveway, her tongue stuck out. Mo pressed her fingers to her temples. The sparrows were acting oddly, fizzing up like feathery bubbles. Not a single bee hovered over Mrs. Steinbott's roses. Mo took her neighbor's porch steps two at a time. In all her years on Fox Street, she'd never done this without permission.

"Good morning, Mrs. Steinbott."

Her porch gleamed. The leaves of her roses shone. Every speck of dirt and dust had been boiled or scrubbed away. Every beetle and blight had been obliterated. On this sterilized porch, the world was in precise, predictable order. Mo looked around longingly. If only she could stay here, safe and solid!

What was she *thinking*? Had she really just wished she could stay with *Starchbutt*?

Who held a piece of white paper, neatly folded and creased.

"I see you got a letter," Mo said.

"Everyone did." She peered at Mo. "What's wrong with you? You don't look right. Oh, no." Her gaze darted across the windswept street. "Did something happen to her? Are they all right?"

"They're fine. They're inside getting ready for some important company. Do you mind if I read your letter?"

"Company?" Without tearing her eyes from Da's porch, Mrs. Steinbott passed Mo the paper.

Mo recognized the stationery at once. The same opening paragraph, introducing himself, blah blah blah. She scanned the page. Here. Right in the center, like the worm in the apple.

"Every indication is that the city is considering tax abatement. . . . Other residents have already accepted this timely offer. . . . Act now to avoid the possibility of the jurisdiction of eminent domain. Avoid legal tangles!"

The words wriggled, wormlike, as she tried to re-read them.

"Could it be?" Mrs. Starchbutt's voice was so low, she must be talking to herself. "Could it be?"

One line squirmed worse than all the rest. Mo told herself she couldn't have read it right.

Other residents have already accepted this timely offer.

Yes, that's what it said. Her heart plummeted. It was

too late. He'd made up his mind.

"You gave her the purse, didn't you?"

"What?" Mo rubbed her eyes. "Um, sure." So what if she hadn't exactly *given* it to Mercedes? Why quibble over small details at a time like this?

"That's good. You're a very good girl."

"Do you mind if I keep this letter?"

Mrs. Steinbott had already turned away and opened her front door. "He was sweet as a climbing rose," she said. "Without the thorns." The door shut quietly behind her.

Mo tried to put the letter in her pocket but realized she was wearing her one and only pair of pocketless shorts. All her others were in the wash.

The wash. She'd left the fur on the shelf beside the machine, where she'd set it when she emptied pockets. In her grogginess, she'd forgotten to take it upstairs and put it in her drawer for safekeeping. As she hurried down the front walk, Pi Baggott coasted by on his skateboard. He flipped up the board, blocking her path.

"What's wrong?"

Mo clenched the letter in her fist. Why did people keep asking what was wrong with her? Nothing was wrong with her—it was the whole entire rest of the world that was wrong.

"Your mother," she accused. "She got a letter about selling your house."

A bee so big and fat it could barely keep aloft bumbled between them, landed on a purple rose, and burrowed in.

"Right—everybody did," said Pi. "Didn't your dad?"

Lies danced on the tip of her tongue—how easy deception had become in the last few weeks. But why should she protect her father? Why pretend he was innocent? He'd taken that crook's offer. He was ready to trade away everything for what he wanted. He was the true traitor.

"My father's been getting letters for weeks."

Pi set his board down and pushed it back and forth with the toe of his shoe. Mo could see him adding up two plus two. The purple rose nodded up and down. "So he knew. Is he the one who already sold?"

How she longed to pour out every last thing to him. What a relief that would be! Instead she stared at the sidewalk.

"My mom says we gotta sell," he went on. "If we don't, the city takes the house anyway and hardly pays us jack."

Pi was a patient person. You could almost hear the

steady *beat beat beat* of his heart as he waited for her to say something. But Mo, it seemed, was only capable of staring at the sidewalk. Mo Wren, moron.

"I think she's wrong, though," Pi said at last. "If you read the letter real careful, it just threatens. Like a punk saying, 'I will freakin' bust your head if you don't give me your jacket.' Like that."

He waited some more and, when Mo still didn't speak, pushed off. Just as quickly he wheeled around. He coasted back, arms at his sides, as if he'd forgotten something. Something of great importance, judging from the serious look he bent on Mo.

"If we have to move," he began. He touched a finger to the purple rose, and the bee shot up and away with an angry hum. "We wouldn't live on the same street anymore."

"You just figured that out? You're really a genius."

If Pi's lips had been about to release a secret, instead they closed around it. Mo watched him zoom up the street, crouch, and leap. Beneath his feet, the board twirled in a perfect 180. In the hazy air Pi hovered as if gravity were a myth. Landing perfectly, he raced away, leaving her in the dust.

The Magic Runs Out

By NOW THE BREEZE had worked itself into a wind, the mischief-making sort that conjures up mini-tornadoes, grabbing bits of trash and grit and whirling them high in the air. Head down, Mo trudged toward her back door. She trailed her fingers along the side of Starchbutt's house, then tossed the wadded-up letter over the fence. But just as she was about to go inside, her ears pricked up. What was that sound, mingling with the wind? A little bark, a musical howl, coming from her own, her very own backyard.

I knew it.

Holding her breath, pressing flat against the house,

Mo crept around the corner. There beneath the plum tree, down on all fours, rusty headed and wild, crouched Dottie, emitting sounds that were a cross between a human's *oh no no no* and an animal's pitiful, wordless wail.

Mo smooshed her forehead against the side of the house. She'd expressly told Dottie she was grounded. The little monster was deliberately disobeying. If there was ever a time Mo was justified in completely and totally letting her sister have it, *kaboom*, now was that time.

But to her own confusion, Mo discovered she had no anger left. She'd used it up, on her father, on Mercedes, on Pi, on the whole world. As enormous as her supply of anger had been, a supply big enough to last a lifetime, it was all gone. Where it had raged and burned was only a hollow tender place, empty as could be.

"What's the matter?" The trickster wind snatched Mo's words away. She crossed the grass to stand over her sister and asked again. Dottie lurched over sideways. Bits of grass stuck to her hands and knees. Around her neck hung a string of plastic pearls Mo had once found tossed down the hill. Dottie claimed they were magic—wearing them gave her X-ray vision.

Oh, if only Mo still believed in magic! If only

she could be as little and ignorant as Dottie, whose world was so simple that just wanting something bad enough might make it happen.

Dottie's hair streamed across her face. When Mo pushed it back, Dottie's cheeks were streaked with tears. All Mo's envy of her little sister vanished. Dottie, who never cried, was crying her head off.

"I'm sorry I yelled at you." Mo tried to pull her sister to her feet. "Let's go inside. You need a bath. I'll let you have bubbles."

But Dottie grabbed her sister's ankle in a death grip. "I didn't mean it," she blubbered.

A strange calm took hold of Mo. She became a smooth rock in a rushing river.

"What? What didn't you mean?"

Dottie looked frightened, like a child who's woken up a guard dog. Mo waited. Calmly. Like a rock.

"How come you never tolded me?" Fat tears rolled down Dottie's cheeks.

"Told you what?"

"Mrs. Petrone gave it to you, right?"

"Gave me what?'

"It was just the same like mine," Dottie bawled. "Everybody says that. You keep saying I don't remember, but I do. I do!"

"Remember *what*?" The river rushing, rising.

Dottie dove forward and buried her head in Mo's lap. "I didn't mean it! I just wanted to look at it for one single tiny minute, and I came out here so you wouldn't know, and I didn't know it was so windy, I didn't know. I didn't mean it!"

Mo dug her fingers into Dottie's hair and yanked her head up. "Where is it? Where is it?"

Dottie's eyes tilted upward in Mo's iron grip. She pointed toward the plum tree, then the house, then the sky, her arm wheeling around like a compass gone loco.

Mo raced around the yard, directionless as the leaves and scraps flying at the mercy of this wind. At the base of the plum tree lay a bit of blue tissue paper, flimsy as a torn moth wing. That was all. By now the weightless fur would have blown everywhere, and nowhere.

"I'll get you some more," Dottie promised. "I'll go ask Mrs. P right now."

"Forget it! You can't!"

"Oh, yeah? Well, she was my mama too!"

Mo spun around. Dottie had her fists up, ready to duke it out.

"Not just yours! Mine too!"

"What are you talking about? That wasn't her hair."

Dottie landed a punch in Mo's belly. "You big fat liar! She wasn't just yours. I remember too!"

Mo caught her arm, but Dottie bared her fangs and bit down on Mo's hand. Hard.

"Yeow!"

Above their heads the branches of the plum tree creaked. Mo, with Dottie still attached, stepped back just as a sudden, sharp crack split the air. A branch swung down and hung there, like a broken arm. A tiny nest spilled onto the grass, then tumbleweeded away.

Dottie's jaw fell open. Mo pressed the back of her hand against her own mouth.

"You bit me."

Instead of apologizing, Dottie put her dukes back up, ready for round two.

"She had a sweater with buttons like Life Savers. She made me dandelion necklaces. I put an ant in my mouth and she took it out and it didn't even die."

"That was fox fur," Mo said. "I found it down in the ravine."

Dottie lowered her fists. How easy it was to read her face—her feelings scrolled across it like closed-captioned TV. Distrust, disappointment, sorrow, guilt.

"Cross your heart?"

Mo longed to say, "I never lie." But that would be a lie.

"I've been looking for signs for a long time," Mo told her. "Every time I go down there, I'm looking."

Lonesomeness flashed across the little face. After all Mo's work to keep her safe, Dottie carried lonesomeness and sorrow around, too. All this time, like a scar in a place no one else ever saw.

"You shoulda showed me, Mo."

"Maybe."

"I'll get you more!"

Laughing and crying—who knew how closely the two were twined inside you?

Mo turned away from her sister and fitted her spine to the trunk of the plum tree—there it was, the groove that had shaped itself, year by year, to cushion and hold her just right. The back of her hand throbbed, and her eyes felt rubbed with sand. The broken branch swung in the wind.

"Don't sit there," Dottie begged. "It's danger out here."

"Just go inside. I'll come in a minute."

"I'm sorry I bited you!"

"Yeah, right."

Dottie looked heartbroken. But what could Mo

do? It was no use. The fur was gone, and with it any power she'd had. Any hope. The fur was scattered on the evil wind, and her father had sold the house, the yard, everything, out from under Mo's feet. All this time she'd believed that if she tried her hardest, and did her best, she could fix things—if one thing didn't work, then something else would, and if not that, then something else. But Mo had run out of things. There was nothing left for her to do.

"Never mind," she said. She longed to make her voice comforting and kind, but Dottie only looked more wretched. What could Mo do? It was no use. The time had come for Dottie to stop believing in magic, stop believing in Mo.

Everything Changes

WHEN MO WOKE, the sky had grown dark, and the very air had changed. She no longer inhabited summer, maybe not even Earth. For one thing, a mangy doll blanket covered her goose-bumpy knees, and for another, her body was experiencing an alien sensation.

The plum leaves shivered, and now Mo did too, as if she'd been paddling along in a warm pond and suddenly found herself in a cold spot. Pond. Swim. Water. That was what Mo was feeling, the long-lost sensation she couldn't put a name to. She was *wet*. It was raining.

Raining! The wind's rough fingers had planted the

air with rain seeds and they were blooming, silver blossoms falling on Fox Street. She watched the rain darken the roofs and the hard, parched ground. As if she herself were a thing with roots, she sensed the plum tree sigh and drink. Up on Paradise, the passing cars made swishing sounds. Mo tilted her head and stuck out her tongue.

Then she remembered. As the rain washed away the world's weary dust, it all came back to her, all the things that had happened and couldn't unhappen. When it arrived at Dottie's secret sadness, Mo's mind snagged and caught.

Yes. There was one thing she might still undo. Wadding up the little doll blanket, she went into the house.

"Dottie! Put on your swimsuit!" Mo shook her head, and drops flew. Glancing at the kitchen clock, she was startled to see how late it was. How long had she slept, after all?

"Dottie! Come on—let's run in the rain together!" She climbed the stairs. "Don't hide. I won't bite you back."

It wasn't as if the Wild Child had never disappeared before. But Mo was surprised she would today, after their big fight, and in this rain. This rain, which was coming down harder and harder, slanting in the windows, wetting the floor and her bed, her bed on which lay a soggy sheet of paper with a strange four-legged creature drawn in orange crayon. The animal wore a big smile, happy as could be in a sea of grass blooming with crooked hearts.

Mo hurried from room to room, shutting windows. In her father's, his Tortilla Feliz softball shirt lay on the bed, and that was when she realized that he hadn't come home in time for his game. It would have started hours ago, before the rain, and when had he ever, ever missed a game? Only one thing she could think of possessed the power to keep him away.

He'd closed the deal. He was buying Corky's, signing away their life once and for all.

The little door inside her opened and banged shut, as if she were a haunted house.

Mo flew back down the stairs. Unable to think straight—would she ever be able to think straight again?—she raced outside. By now the rain was pouring down so hard, she could barely see Mercedes's house. Even Dottie wouldn't stay out in this! She must have ducked inside someone's house. Grabbing an umbrella, Mo dashed down the steps.

None of the Baggotts had seen her since morning.

As Mo thanked them and headed back into the rain, Pi raced after her. He threw a yellow poncho over her head. It stunk, but the rain rolled off it like a duck's back.

"Thanks."

Pi had already forgotten how mean she'd been to him. Or else he was as good at forgiveness as he was at kick flips. He headed toward Paradise, shouting over his shoulder, "I'll check out Abdul's and E-Z Dollar!"

Mr. Duong, glasses misting over, interrogated Mo. Did Dottie know not to cross Paradise on her own? Not to talk to strangers? She wouldn't go down the ravine when it was storming like this, would she? That stream could flash flood. How long had she been missing?

"She's not missing. She's just . . . not here."

Mr. Duong patted her rubbery shoulder. "Right. Don't worry now," he said, looking exceedingly worried. "I'll notify the authorities."

Mrs. Petrone leaned over the railing of her porch, calling Mo up.

"You think you're a duck?" She produced a slightly hairy towel and rubbed Mo's head.

"I'm looking for Dottie." Mo swallowed down her

rising fear. "I don't guess she's here?"

"I saw her run by a while ago, but I didn't pay attention. That letter has me so distracted!" Mrs. Petrone shook out the towel. "Somebody already struck a deal—it must be those shady people in the old Kowalski house, don't you think?" Mrs. Petrone broke off, noticing Mo's face. "*Bella*, what am I doing? Here you are worried to death about your baby sister while I go on and on about money! What does that matter, compared to that girl?"

"I'm not worried, I'm just . . . Yes, I am, Mrs. P. I'm really, really worried!"

"Calm down, catch your breath, that's it. Now tell me, where's that handsome father of yours?"

"I don't know!"

Mrs. Petrone frowned, then crushed Mo to her coconut-scented chest.

"Poor dear man! He has so much to worry about, it's not right!"

"I need him!" Mo's words got swallowed up in the squashy soft folds of Mrs. P's front. "He should be here!"

"With that red hair, she can't hide for long! We'll find her! Next thing you know, the two of you will be sitting on my porch having milk and pizzelles."

Mo's throat closed, and for a moment she was afraid she'd throw up. She dashed back out into the storm.

Mrs. Steinbott's grass was littered with the petals of roses shattered by the force of the rain. No one home at the Tortilla Feliz house, or the old Kowalski house, and that left Da's.

"Hello?" she called through the screen door. "Hello?" The rain pounding on the porch roof drowned out her voice. Mo turned away, then forced herself to pull open the door and step inside. "Hello?"

Mercedes's head appeared around the living-room doorway. She wore another outfit Mo had never seen before—a flowered skirt cut like a frothy little bubble, with matching leggings and tank top. In her hands she held one of Da's big black shoes. Her eyes rounded at the sight of the yellow tent planted in the hallway.

Though she already knew the answer, Mo squeaked, "Is Dottie here?"

"Mo Wren?"

Da sat on the couch in a beautiful lilac pantsuit, wearing one shoe. Mo's eyes darted away. Mercedes must have been helping Da with her special stockings and shoes—they were getting ready for Cornelius and Monette's visit. Neither said a word about Mo's

176

muddy feet on the clean carpet.

And then Mo noticed something else. Starchbutt's pocketbook was propped up on a cushion beside Da, almost like another person sitting there. A guest of honor. Mo had been certain Mercedes would toss that thing straight in the trash.

"Never mind," Mo said. "She's not here, and you're busy." She spun away, but Da commanded her to halt, then demanded to hear everything, from Dottie getting in big trouble, to their terrible fight, to Mo falling asleep, to all the places Mo had searched.

"But she wouldn't go far, not in this rain, would she?" Mercedes asked, then smacked her forehead. "What am I talking about? She's Dottie."

"How did she get in trouble?" Da asked.

"She . . . she took something of mine. I shouldn't have made such a big deal out of it." If only she hadn't! "But . . . it meant a lot to me."

Da's face turned gentle. "That's why she wanted it, Mo Wren." She fingered the clasp on Starchbutt's purse. "You're the sun and the moon to that child, and rightly so."

"I'm so scared! She went into the ravine, I just know it. She'll get lost. She never thinks ahead. She never thinks! It flash floods and she can't swim. She thinks

177

she can, but . . . and if she makes it to the Metropark, anything could happen."

"Give me strength," said Da. "What are you waiting for, Mercedes Jasmine?"

"Right, we're wasting time." Mercedes ducked out of the room and returned wearing a cool jacket with a million pockets. She Velcroed her cell phone into one. "Let's go."

Mo stared. "You're coming?"

"No. I'm going to a fashion show. Come on!"

"But . . . Cornelius!"

"Stuff Cornelius!" exclaimed Mercedes, and astonishingly, Da did not correct her. Instead she thumped her cane on the carpet.

"You find that child and bring her back here lickety-split, so we can hug her hard, then scold her within an inch of her precious life." She thumped the cane again. "Oh, I'd give anything to come with you."

Da struggled to her feet, and Mo knew she meant it. Toeless and weak as she was, she had the courage of ten Mos! Disgust with herself made Mo shudder. What kind of weenie was she, anyway? If Da could live with those stumpy mutilated feet, Mo could at least summon the bravery to look at them.

Da's lap, Da's knees, Da's ankles. And then . . . Da's

foot, with the gaping empty places like sockets without eyes, just as painful and ugly looking as Mo had feared.

And Da was standing upright on them, all by herself.

"We'll find her." Mercedes kissed her grandmother's cheek. She paused to let her eyes rest on the purse, as if it truly were another person she had to tell good-bye, don't you worry.

Then they ran out into the storm.

Into the Storm

THE HILL WAS A WATER SLIDE. Hardened as the ground was, the rain shot off it in sheets. By the time they reached the Den, Mercedes's beautiful skirt was a sodden, muddy disaster. She stepped out of it, then tossed it on top of the toolbox.

"That's better," she said. "Now I'm streamlined for action."

They shouted.

"Dottie! Dottie! Dottie!"

"The rain's so loud."

"So are we."

"Dottieeeeee! Dottieeeeee!"

Mo was so accustomed to being quiet in these woods, to making herself as invisible as she could, it was hard to force her voice out into the air. She imagined the mother fox, watching from her den. *So. She's just one of them, after all. Just another loud, stupid human blundering around here, making trouble. She'll never get a look at us, that's for sure.*

"It's my sister," she told the hillside. "I have to find her."

Mercedes spun around. "What?"

"Why was I so mean to her, Merce? All those times I forced her to wear underwear. And last night I locked her out of my room."

Mercedes planted both feet firmly, the way Da did, which was a considerable challenge on that slick slope.

"Sometimes mean is the only way you can go. I should know." She wiped her streaming face with the hem of her jacket. "And that reminds me. What do you know about that handbag?"

"I was keeping it. I knew it'd freak you."

"You were right."

Inside her rubber tent, Mo grew very warm. She flapped her arms a little.

"You think I only see the up side of things. But Starchbutt's not that bad. She's almost kind of . . ." She was going to say "cute," but she could already hear Mercedes replying, *Yeah, cute like a tarantula. Like a rabid vampire bat.*

But Mercedes didn't even notice Mo hadn't finished her sentence.

"There was something strange inside it," she said. "At first I couldn't understand what it was. I mean, I knew what it was, but I didn't know why it was. So I showed Da. She took one look and said, '*Aah.*' " Mercedes tilted her face, aiming that Walcott chin toward heaven.

Mo squinted upward, trying to see what Mercedes did.

"I've heard of messages in a bottle," Mercedes went on. "But never a message in a handbag."

In this weather you couldn't tell the difference between rain and tears. Mercedes wiped her cheeks. "It's so weird. It's like . . . like all my atoms and molecules somehow got rearranged, not to mention my DNA, and I've been turned into a different person."

"You look the same."

Mercedes shook her head. "Don't, Mo." It wasn't a lecturing, I-know-better-than-you voice. It was a quiet, truth-speaking voice. "I'm not."

What wasn't Mercedes telling her? Whatever the secret was, it felt as enormous as this storm, but Mo had lost the right to demand an answer from her former best friend. The only reason Mercedes had come on this search party at all was because Da was so worried about Dottie. She wasn't doing this for Mo's sake, that was certain. Outside her poncho, the rain streamed down, and inside it, Mo began to sweat. What was in the purse? Something that had changed Mercedes's life yet again. To think she'd almost thrown it away, in her fury at Mercedes for not being Mercedes anymore!

But then Mercedes said, "Come here."

They huddled inside the Den, out of the rain. It was cooler in there, and misty, so when Mercedes un-Velcroed one of her jacket's many pockets and drew something out, she seemed to be pulling it out of another place, or time, altogether. She handed it to Mo. A photo. Its colors hadn't held up, and the two people in it, and the air all around them, basked in an unreal, orangey glow. A pale young man in an army uniform, holding himself very straight, had his arm around a beautiful woman who held her chin just so. Da in her younger days? Merce in the future? Mo's brain tilted.

Monette. That's who it had to be. She stood a head taller than the army guy and clasped a big purse. Even though they both looked right into the camera, you could tell their smiles were really for each other.

Inside Mo, a thought began to stir and stretch, like a beautiful animal waking up.

"It was in his things," said Mercedes. "From the

military. The stuff they sent home after he died. She only opened it this summer. More than ten years later. She says she never . . . never had the heart before."

The message in the handbag.

"We think it was the day he left for the service," Mercedes said. "A friend must have taken it."

Mo looked more closely at the handsome, kindly-eyed man in the photo.

"He and Monette always liked each other, all the way back to when they were little, but she . . . his . . ." Mercedes faltered. "Da says Mrs. Steinbott never wanted them playing together. My mother was always into so much mischief, and he hated upsetting his mother. He was all she had. Da says he was as obedient and sweet as Monette was wild. And it wasn't as if Da encouraged them to be friends. She's so proud— she never really forgave Mrs. Steinbott for snubbing her all those years." Mercedes wiped her eyes again. "They're two of a kind, really."

Mo gazed down at the photo. Even though the colors had faded, she could tell his eyes had been blue, like chips of sky.

"He . . . he looks nice, Merce. He looks really nice."

Mercedes seemed to be trying to decide if what Mo said was true.

"He never knew. About me. We figured it out. He died too soon."

All these years she'd thought her father had taken off and never looked back, when the truth was, he'd never even known about her. Which hurt more? Was this good news or bad news?

"I can't believe it," Mercedes whispered. "I mean . . . she's my . . ."

"Grandmother."

Mercedes nodded.

Outside the Den, the rain fell harder yet, sheets and sheets of it, so you could hardly tell the sky from the ground. The world had lost its up and down. It had no back and front, no now and then, no them and us. At this moment, Fox Street itself was probably no longer a road but a river, solid turned liquid.

"She's been trying to tell me all summer, in her own loony way," Mercedes said. "And I just kept running away. Chances are excellent that if it weren't for you being so nice all the time, I still wouldn't know."

Mercedes took the photo back and carefully slid it into her pocket. She fastened the Velcro, then held her hand over it a moment.

"Come on," she said at last, and ducked back out into the wind, Mo right behind her.

Match Flame

THEY CLIMBED DOWN, down, past flattened cans
and rusty wire, a bicycle tire and a plastic cemetery
wreath, down past the invisible line where the trash
ended and the real kingdom began.

The sound of rushing water grew louder, as if a
twin storm had blown up. The farther down they
went, the louder it became, till at last they came to
the spot where the hill gave out. Nearly erased a day
ago, now the stream rushed and leaped, foaming
over rocks, whipping fallen leaves and sticks along
on a wild ride.

They both stood and stared.

Water overflowed the banks. There was nothing for it but to drop straight down into the stream. The moment Mo's feet hit, she lost her balance and toppled forward, landing on her knees. The water rushed nearly as high as her shoulders. Mercedes gave her a hand, and holding on to each other, they battled across to the far side of the stream.

How would Dottie ever make it?

"You see any footprints?"

But the water was rising so rapidly, any traces would be wiped out within minutes. It sloshed in Mo's sneakers, streamed into her eyes. Water had taken over the world, wiping out, washing away. The thicket where she'd found the fox fur was only a dozen feet away, yet she could hardly see it.

Dottie would plunge straight in. She'd never guess how deep it was. How strong the current. Though maybe, when she'd come down here, the stream hadn't been this swollen. Mo tried to catch her breath.

"What's that?"

From underneath a bush, Mercedes pulled out a sparkly purple sandal. Its stiff plastic strap jutted up, torn through at the buckle. A moment later, she came up with its mate.

Mo's relief gave way to new worry as she imagined

her sister soaked from head to foot. Barefoot.

"This is good," Mercedes tried to convince her. "It'll slow her down."

But all Mo could see was her sister's small pink feet, scraped and wounded. And now she found herself remembering Da's feet. Mo's courage began to fail.

"Mo," Mercedes said, her voice firm and solemn. "We have to split up. She made it across the stream— there's no stopping her. She could've gone anywhere, in any direction."

Small as Dottie was, when she was determined there was no stopping her. Mo knew Mercedes was right. Yet the idea of searching all by herself made her go cold to the bone.

All alone! Sorrow and anger and fear crowded up inside her. Why wasn't he here? He was supposed to be here! But he didn't even know what was happening. He didn't care about the things that really mattered. He made big mistakes, he chose the wrong things, he left them to fend for themselves.

Mo stared up into the dark, tree-choked sky. Someone had torn a jagged hole across it. *I'll never trust you again as long as I live!* The words flared up inside her, like a match struck in an unlit room. Then *poof!* The match burned out, leaving her alone in the unknowable darkness. Mo put her arms around herself, a tent inside a tent. Wind rattled the trees.

Mercedes stood patiently, practically in her underwear, coated with mud, water dripping off her sensitive nose. Was she really here only because of Da? She hadn't had to show Mo the photo. She'd trusted Mo. She'd wanted Mo to know.

"Ready?" Mercedes asked her. "Because I am."

"We're friends again, aren't we."

Mercedes wrinkled that persnickety nose. "Only if you swear never to wear that poncho again."

The Thinker, Part 3

HEADS TOGETHER, they forged a plan. Mercedes would head toward the parking lot, then search the picnic grounds and vicinity. Mo, who knew the hillside and stream area so well, would continue hunting here, in case Dottie wandered in circles and wound up back where she started. In an hour, no matter what, they'd meet at the Den.

Mo's best friend parted the solid sheet of rain and disappeared.

"Dottie! Dottie!"

No sooner did Mo send the syllables up than they tumbled back down, landing in the mud. Her throat ached from shouting. Her feet tangled in a vine.

At the thicket where she'd found the fur, rain glazed the thorns, making them shine like tiny daggers.

I need you.

Blindly, dully, Mo retraced her footsteps. She sloshed back across the stream, climbed halfway up the hill, slipping and sliding in the muddy tracks she'd made herself, only a few minutes before.

Stop, Mo. A voice that was both hers and not hers whispered inside her. *You can do better than this.*

Mo pressed her fingers to her temples.

Think. Think like Dottie.

Dottie, with her big heart and small self. Her bare feet and short legs. By now she'd be all worn out. Lemme take a little rest, she'd think. She'd plop down, she'd pull a snack out of her pocket. . . .

As if Mo's brain had conjured it, a waxy bit of paper blew against her feet. A Dum-Dum wrapper. Sour apple.

Mo opened her mouth to shout—but instead she listened.

Ssssh, whispered the voice inside her. *Gently.*

Mo stood very still.

Patiently. You know how.

Mo pulled the bright, alarming poncho off and

laid it on the ground. Rain wet her in the few places she was still dry, evening her out, making her just the same as the trees, the grasses, the glazed thicket.

Yes, whispered the voice. *That's better.*

One cautious step at a time, zigzagging to avoid jutting stones, fallen branches, slumps of rotting leaves. To one side lay the racing stream. The wind gusted.

Mo hadn't ventured this far into the kingdom all summer. Another powerful storm had swept through here, maybe in the spring. The trees were battered, missing limbs. The spots where they'd broken off were still raw looking, like the gaps on Da's feet. Some trees had taken their neighbors down with them when they fell, crashing to the ground tangled in each other's woody arms. Mo stepped carefully, feeling the air grow warmer. Without the thick cover of leaves, the sun would be more generous here. It would pour out great, golden buckets, and that was why the wild mustard and the first black-eyed Susans were already blooming here, and why those black raspberries were plump and ripe.

Berries. Sweet, smeary, eat-till-your-greedy-little-belly-busts berries.

Slowly. You know how.

The voice filled Mo, the way the joy of her father's

singing did, or the perfume of Mrs. Steinbott's roses, filled her with something she couldn't name, something that nuzzled her, assured her, carried her forward.

How easily her feet navigated the ground. No twigs snapped. No vines or prickers snagged. The rain began to fall more softly, its thick gray curtain turning pearly and translucent.

The voice was both inside and outside her now.

Just ahead lay a majestic, fallen tree, its bark thick and protective as the shingles on a house. This tree had fallen long before the others. Grass sprang up around it, and silver-green moss grew a furry coat along its ridges. Just beyond it, a tangle of pale purple berry canes snagged the light. The thick clusters of berries appeared lit up from inside, as if each one cupped its own tiny candle. Mo stopped, her heart beating patiently, steadily.

Here you are. At last.

From the other side of the log, the fox raised her head, unsurprised, and gazed at Mo. Her face was long and narrow, her delicate ears tipped forward in greeting. Her red fur was wet and matted, as if she'd been waiting a long time.

I knew you'd come.

The fur at the base of her throat glowed white as a star. Her almond-shaped eyes held Mo's in a look both loving and searching.

The fox stretched her neck and nuzzled the air. Nothing, nothing about her was frightening. Mo longed to run toward her. Her arms lifted, aching to circle that neck, to press her cheek against its downy warmth.

But as if she could read Mo's mind, the fox rose up on all fours. She bent her face to something on the ground, hidden from Mo's sight. The fox's eyes slowly closed, their light winking out, her beautiful self drawing in, motionless and rapt, as if trying to memorize this moment. Mo didn't dare breathe. She hung suspended, willing this moment to last forever.

But already time was up. A flash of velvet black legs, and the white-tipped tail streamed out like something in your happiest dream. No one could keep up with her, even in a dream, but just before she disappeared into the undergrowth, she stopped. She looked back with those wise eyes only a shade darker than her fur, eyes that saw so many things you couldn't.

Foxes and humans can't mix. That's how life is. But wherever we both go, we'll remember.

Swift, silent, an arrow shot from an invisible bow. She was gone.

Mo bent over the fallen tree's thick, ridged walls. She held her hand over the spot where the fox had been, cupping the lingering warmth in her palm. Cradled against the tree, nearly hidden, something else stirred. A small wild animal uncurled and sat up, yawning and rubbing her eyes with her fists. At the sight of Mo bending over her, Dottie smiled dreamily.

"You said I couldn't, but I did. Lookit!" Dottie opened a fist sticky with mashed berries, and there, right in the center, like her heart in her body or their house in the center of the street, lay a tuft of hair that at first looked transparent. But then a slender beam of pale, watery sun caught it, and the fur turned just the same color as Dottie's hair. She looked from it to her big sister and then back again, her sleepy, berry-streaked face coming fully awake, alive with wonder.

Wren Den

DOTTIE CONTENTEDLY SIPPED the last can of Tahitian Treat, while outside, the world dripped away the last raindrops. The sound of the swollen stream played beneath the voices of the birds as they began to sing again. Mo had retrieved the poncho and spread it on the ground, and dried Dottie's scraped-up feet with a bit of old towel. Dottie had sworn she never got lost, not for a single minute, and then she'd cried a little bit, and then Mo had given her the last can of pop, and now she was all right again.

She'd almost gotten scared, Dottie said, but then she found a trail. It was a nice little trail all mooshed down so it didn't hurt her feet at all, and it led right straight smack to the berries. And that was when she found the fur. And that was when she got so sleepy, like someone had put a dream spell on her.

Birdsongs stitched the trees together with trembling, silvery threads. Mo knew she should tell Dottie about the fox. But oh, she was glad her little sister hadn't seen it. The secret still belonged to her alone.

"Daddy's going to be mad at me, right?" Dottie asked.

Mo watched a raindrop slide to the tip of a branch, hang on as long as it could, then let go and plummet. "He doesn't even have a clue you were missing."

"You're mad at him, right?" Dottie sighed. "Everybody's so mad all the time."

Water dripping, birds singing, the sideways waterfall of the brimming stream—she tried to listen past all that waterlogged clamor for any sign of Mercedes. It had been more than an hour. Mo hated thinking of her best friend still searching. She knew Mercedes would rather die than give up and come back alone. Mercedes! How could Mo ever have doubted her?

"I had a dream," Dottie began, her voice dreamy.

But now a new, powerful sound bored straight through all the others, like a train in a tunnel.

"Mo!" The deep, anguished bellow came from above instead of below. "Mo! Dottie!"

The Wild Child went off like a firecracker.

"Daddy!"

Arms and legs wheeling, she exploded out of the Den. Mo watched as, a dozen yards up the hill, he clasped Dottie to him like he'd never let go.

"Are you all right? Dottie, Little Speck, thank God . . ."

"I bited Mo. And my shoe busted. I couldn't help it."

"I'll buy you new shoes. I'll buy you ten pairs of shoes!" Mr. Wren promised, making Dottie laugh. "A hundred pairs!"

To Mo's confusion, he wore his water department uniform. When he saw her, his whole self seemed to open out—Mo thought of one of Mrs. Steinbott's roses. It was all she could do not to run to him, too, and bury her face in that flung-wide sweetness. Instead she wrapped her arms tight around herself and stood her ground, while her father staggered down the hill like a man with one leg shorter than the other, Dottie in his arms.

"This is Mo and Mercey's clubhouse, Daddy. It's secret and pirate and we're not allowed."

Mr. Wren set Dottie on her feet. He bear-hugged

Mo, who managed to keep herself stiff as one of Mrs. Steinbott's boiled sponges.

"I get home and the whole street's in an uproar. Duong's got half the police force out, the Baggotts are plastering LOST signs all over Paradise." He looked at Dottie, who was fussing around inside the Den. "They're offering a million-dollar reward for you, Little Bit." His voice choked off.

"Come on in," invited Dottie. She'd found Mercedes's discarded skirt and pulled it on, and now she made a sweeping gesture, like a TV game-show hostess. "Take a load off."

Bent in half, Mr. Wren backed into the Den. He lowered himself onto a beanbag like a man who'd been waiting to rest a long time.

"So I ran to Da's, and she knew right where you . . . Da!" He pulled out his phone and hit speed dial. "Got her!" he said into it, and Mo could hear Da's "Lord give me strength!" all the way from where she stood outside the Den door.

"Yeah, she was with Mo, where else would she be?" he said into the phone. "Safe and sound, safe as can be. . . . Mercedes?" He broke off, listening. "You didn't hear from her? Don't worry—it must be she can't get a signal, that's all. Hey, we're not coming back without her! I'll call you right away. She'll be all right—she's a Walcott. Don't worry." Clicking off, he regarded Mo with wonder.

"Just how long were you out here searching?"

Mo lifted her chin, making herself into a righteous steeple. He must have forgotten she wasn't speaking to him.

"Long, huh? Really long."

Long as the Mississippi, thought Mo. Her father hung his weary head.

"What a day," he said. "Between the storm and that busted main, I know how that sucker Noah felt. After wishing for rain half the summer, I saw enough water to sink the *Titanic*. I—"

"Wait," said Mo, the first word she'd spoken to him in days and days. "Another main broke? That's where you were?"

Mr. Wren looked up, gaping. "Where'd you think I was? I left a note, didn't . . ." He slapped his pockets, as if it might be in there. "Shoot. I didn't, did I? Forgot my phone, too."

Mo inched closer. "You weren't signing the papers?"

Mr. Wren rubbed the tree trunk between his eyes. Its outline was so sharp and deep, Mo winced to see it. "I was at work. Yeah, work. I'm sorry, Mo.

I should have been here."

"But . . . I thought you were with Buckman. Or signing the papers for Corky's."

Mr. Wren's head snapped up. Sharp little waves of anger came crashing off him. "Why are you standing out there?" he demanded. "How am I supposed to talk to you when you're so far away?"

Mo edged inside. Carefully she sat on the other beanbag, hands in her lap.

"And why are you bringing that Buckmeister up now?" he wanted to know.

"Because." Mo stiffened her spine. "I saw a letter that said somebody already sold out, and the rest of the street has no choice. They have to sell or else."

His laugh was short and hard, like a rock thrown at a brick wall. "What an operator. You've got to admire the guy."

"Admire!" she sputtered. "Him?"

His look was furious. Mo's heart felt lumpy inside her, like something that had melted, then hardened wrong.

"After I took you to see Corky's, I went to the library and pulled up some past reports on B and B."

Mr. Wren ground his fist into his hand, as if trying to break in a new mitt.

"Their history ain't pretty. They bought up land in Florida, cleared it, and then when the financing fell through, they flat-out abandoned the project. All in a day's work, I guess. It sure didn't discourage Buckman from trying the same thing with our neighborhood."

"He's mean!" hooted Dot.

"Naaah. He's human." Mr. Wren socked the invisible mitt one more time, then leaned back on his elbows. How exhausted he looked. "It's a cold, cruel world out there, every greedy man for himself. If that guy can make things happen fast enough, he doubles his money on our house and everybody else's. He'll make a bundle turning a pig's ear into a Gucci purse, then retire to Florida himself."

The look on his face was dark as the bottom of a well. He thought the world was a cold, narrow place, the only light a little pinprick far out of reach. Believing that was doing him in. It was crushing him flat. In spite of herself, Mo longed to cheer him up. In spite of herself, she slid a little closer. And broke a little clod of mud off his work shoe. Because here they were, the three of them. Somehow, in the middle of the woods, in the worst of storms, each of them wandering around confused and mistaken, somehow they'd found one another.

Mo looked out the door of the Den. The world was silver and slippery. All right, it was true—you couldn't stop bad things from happening. No human got that kind of power, no matter how you longed and wished for it. But if you knew how to look, if you knew how to listen, if you knew when to hunt and when to wait, you'd find the good things. They'd show themselves. They'd come.

Mo and her fox had memorized each other. A part of Mo had slipped off into the beautiful, mysterious kingdom, and a part of the fox was here, nuzzling them, keeping them together.

Mo turned to her father, who was looking so sad and angry her lumpy heart ached. *You're wrong*, Mo yearned to tell him. *Or you're only partway right.* But if she told him so, he'd tell her to quit thinking so much.

That was all right. Mo loved him too much not to try.

"Daddy," she began.

"It'll kill me to let that money go," he told her.

"I know."

"But it'd kill me even worse to do business with that bush leaguer. Give me a dozen busted mains before I turn over the most valuable thing we own to a guy like him."

Mo sat back, dazzled and confused as if he'd just shone a bright light in her face.

"You." He pointed at her. "You're the one. You had to go and put second thoughts in my thick head. If it wasn't for you, that house would be signed, sealed, and delivered, and I'd be one happy if ignorant man."

His fingernails were caked with dirt. At the back of his head shone a round bald spot the size of a penny. Where had that come from?

"But Daddy, the letter said somebody did sell to him."

"Trust me. The only house he's bought so far is the one they tore down."

"But what about eminent domain?"

"Is that in the letter, too? Forget about it. He doesn't have a prayer of getting the city to declare it. Apparently there's nothing that greedy lard butt won't stoop to, including twisting the truth."

Suddenly he grinned, his eyes gleaming like dark stars. Oh, he was handsome. The handsomest man on Fox Street, probably in the entire city.

"Easy come, easy go. Did Shakespeare say that?" He sighed. Little by little, the light faded from his eyes.

He wasn't selling. They were staying. All because of her.

"Hey." Mr. Wren poked her knee. "You don't exactly look like a girl who just got what she wanted."

"I . . . I'm happy. I'm sad, too."

"What'd I tell you? You think too much."

"I want us all to be happy, Daddy. Together."

"That's a bigger order than we thought, isn't it?"

Mo nodded.

Mr. Wren sat up, resting his elbows on his knees. "I won't lie. I'm not giving up on the Wren House. I mean, the Wren House number two. I'm going to have it, sooner or later." He looked at Mo for a long moment. "What would you say to sooner?"

Outside the Den, the honeyed sunlight drizzled down, coating the branches of the trees and spilling over the gray rocks.

"We can put the house up for sale ourselves. It's ours. We'll do it on our terms, and make sure we get a good price, and good people." He touched her cheek. "It's time, Mojo. Good things are ahead, I feel it."

Mo didn't trust her voice.

"What do you say?" her father asked. "Can I still count on you for my manager?"

But her heart. She did trust that, and she heard what it was telling her now. Mo drew a breath. She nodded.

Mr. Wren tried for a fist bump but instead grabbed Mo's hand.

"Hey! What bit you?"

"Grrr," growled Dottie, attacking him from behind. She threw her arms around his neck. "I'm a fox. Grrr."

Mr. Wren wrestled her over his shoulder.

"You know how I always say the only thing that could make me happy was being my own boss? I was wrong. Hard as that is to believe." He tickled Dottie's bare foot. "There's one other thing, and that's being the best dad you two ever had."

Mo's unbalanced heart tipped her sideways, into the jumble of arms and mud and Wren-ness. The three of them fit just right in this den. We could live here, she thought. We could rig up a real roof, and come winter we'd build a thick wall from logs, and chink it up with mud and leaves. We'd cook on a fire, and wash clothes in the stream. I'd gather us berries. We could live here. We could live any—

Mercedes's voice called in the distance. All three of them shouted back, a deafening chorus.

And One More Gift, Part 2

THE STREET SHONE like a black mirror. The dust was gone, and the neighborhood was drenched in color, a page in the coloring book of someone who pressed down hard on her crayons. Headed for the horizon, the sun gleamed like a polished coin.

"Still not here," Mercedes said, pointing toward Da's empty driveway.

Monette and Three-C. Mo had forgotten all about them.

"Don't worry," she promised Mercedes. "When they get here, I'll be right beside you. Two against two!"

But even as she said them, the words sounded

wrong. In families it couldn't ever truly be *against*. Maybe *beside*, or *among*, or *in between*. Maybe even *without*. But *against*, that wouldn't work, not for long.

Mercedes's long, muddy legs took Da's front steps two at a time. She disappeared inside. Except for the rainwater gurgling into the drains, the street was quiet as a stage after the play has ended. Or just before it begins.

"You know what?" Mr. Wren hoisted Dottie onto his shoulders. "I could eat a horse."

Pi was the first to spot them. He Paul Revered down the street on his board, calling out, "She's saved! The Wild Child is back!" Dottie waved and blew kisses as people spilled out onto their porches.

"You found her," Pi told Mo. He flipped up his board to hold it by an axle. "Why am I not surprised?"

His hair was soaking wet. He must have been searching this whole time.

"I forgot your poncho down the hill," she said.

He shrugged. "Keep it."

Mo lowered her eyes, focusing on his reconstituted board, now painted a deep, dark blue. "You know this morning, when you asked me if we were moving . . ."

Pi set the board down and hopped back on, fingers

tucked in his armpits. "Wait a minute. That was this morning?"

It did seem like days ago.

"Well. Guess what." Mo drew a breath. "We are."

She felt as if she'd been holding a heavy box all by herself and could at last put it down. Her arms ached with emptiness, but there was relief, too.

"When?"

"Not yet. But we will."

"Not yet is cool."

"You think?"

From the Baggotts' yard came the pop of leftover Fourth of July firecrackers.

"Gives you time to learn how to skateboard. Right?"

Before she could answer, Pi turned toward his house.

"Okay!" she yelled after him. "It's a deal!"

"Mojo!" Mr. Wren swooped Dottie down off his shoulders. "I'm going to Abdul's! Be right back!"

With the rain over, and Dottie safe and sound, people seemed reluctant to go back inside. Ms. Hugg brought her keyboard out onto her porch and began to noodle out some music. Baby Baggott took off down the sidewalk butt naked, and somehow Mrs. Baggott, flip-flopping behind him, wound up on Mrs. Petrone's porch getting a hair consult. Mo watched Mr. Duong roll his grill into his driveway and get a fire going.

The couple from the Kowalskis' old house, who worked the night shift, must have had the day off. They came outside and stood blinking like bewildered night creatures. Mrs. Hernandez, hand extended, crossed the street to them.

"Hey, where's the party?" A couple of guys from the Tip Top, red cheeked and way too happy, wandered down to lean against a parked car.

Dottie raced by with a tall, empty green bottle. "His name's Brad."

The dips in the sidewalk brimmed with rain. Sparrows hopped from puddle to puddle, excited as little kids on opening day at the pool. From the ground rose a soft mist, wrapping the houses and bushes, smudging corners, blurring the edges of things. The sweet smell of hickory smoke mixed with wet grass and steamy sidewalk.

By now nearly everyone was out. Only Mrs. Steinbott's door was shut tight, her porch graveyard quiet. That wasn't right.

Mo crossed the street, meaning to knock on her door, but somehow kept on going, up the driveway, into the backyard, to stand beneath the plum tree.

210

The tree's broken branch hung down, motionless now the wind had stopped. Mo touched the raw place where it had cracked off, and then, lifting the branch, she tried to fit it back into place. No sooner did she let go than it swung loose, and this time it came away altogether, falling to the ground among the sad, unripe fruit.

But in a sudden rush of wings, a blackbird flapped by, circled, and sat on a branch above her. *Squawk.* It drew Mo's eye to a cluster of plums that had managed, despite the drought, to grow to nearly normal size. Mo realized she was hungry enough to eat a horse herself. Up on her toes, she picked one, then bit into its dusky skin. Not sweet as it should be, but good enough. Mo picked another one and ate that, too. Just as she was about to toss the pits on the ground, the bossy bird cried out again, and Mo remembered the backyard of Corky's, and that restless cardinal looking for a place to settle. That sorry yard, not a tree to its name, blank as a piece of paper no one ever bothered to write on. *Squawk!* The blackbird fixed her with a round, knowing eye.

And here came another one of Mo's thoughts.

She wiped the slimy, golden stones on the leg of her wet shorts and carried them inside. Down in the basement she pulled a pair of shorts from the laundry she'd done just this morning, a hundred years ago, and changed into them. Upstairs she carefully sealed the twin pits inside a Baggie, slid it into her pocket, and gave it a pat. How did people live without pockets? She pictured Mercedes sealing that astonishing photo safe and snug inside her jacket pocket.

Mercedes. Mo couldn't wait to tell her her new idea. But first she had to make sure Mrs. Steinbott was all right.

What a day! Drawing a deep breath, she headed back outside. Along the fence, around the corner of the house, past the roses. To the foot of the steps leading to Mrs. Steinbott's porch.

Where Mo stopped. And rubbed her eyes.

Dark and light, tall and minuscule. They sat side by side in the porch chairs like queens of opposing kingdoms who had, at last, crossed the wide river dividing them and shaken hands. Just behind them stood the peace treaty herself. Mercedes.

"There you are," she said to Mo.

Dusk nibbled at the edges of the street, where Taur Baggott darted by, emitting his spooky alien noise. A smooth melody rippled out from Ms. Hugg's. Mo's father, back from the store, had commandeered Mr.

Duong's grill and was busy flipping burgers and turn-ing brats. "Bush leaguer!" Mo heard him exclaim, and she knew he was telling everyone what he'd found out about Buckman. Mrs. Baggott dragged lawn chairs out into the street, while Mrs. Petrone spread a flow-ered cloth over a picnic table. Voices rose, people laughed.

"Come on," said Mercedes. "We've been waiting for you."

Out on Fox Street, the jubilant commotion rolled on. Up here on Starchbutt's porch, a small, still space opened out.

Mrs. Steinbott's little claw reached for Mo's hands. "See? I've got . . . I've got family."

Mo nodded, and Mrs. Steinbott's fingers curled tight over hers.

Da reached across the space between them and caught up Mrs. Steinbott's other hand.

"We mean to make up for all that time we fool-ishly wasted." Da shook her head. "Come to discover Gertrude and I have both had our notions, all these years. Thinking back, we've both come this close to the truth." Her long fingers signified a tiny pinch. "But we shied away. Isn't it funny how you can know something and refuse to know it at the same time?"

Mo nodded again. It was exactly how, at this very moment, she felt about Fox Street. Look at it! So familiar and so unknown at the same time.

Da tugged Mercedes close. The four of them made a circle as lumpy and hopeful as one that a little kid might draw.

"Too. Good." Mrs. Steinbott swallowed, watery blue eyes glittering. "You! You made this happen!"

Da beamed at Mo.

"Her name's Mo Wren," she said. "But what's in a name? That which we call a rose by any other name would smell as sweet."

The (Dead) End

THE EVENING MIST wreathed Fox Street in a delicious coolness the likes of which it hadn't felt for weeks. Everyone had eaten barbecue till they were ready to burst, and now Mrs. P was pressing pizzelles on people. Walking through the near dark toward the Green Kingdom, Mo heard a car horn toot and turned to watch a big silver car nose its way down the street. Three-C, it had to be. What would he make of Mercedes coated in mud, and Baby Baggott's diaperless butt, and the guys from the Tip Top dancing in the street? And what about Monette? What would she do when she discovered Da, Mrs. Steinbott, and

Mercedes all waiting for her? Maybe she'd already decided to tell her secret. Maybe that was what she'd come to tell Merce, the reason she'd come home at last. Mo hoped so. Any minute now, there was going to be a whole lot of exclaiming and explaining and crying and laughing up on that spotless Steinbott porch.

Mo knew she'd hear all about it, first thing tomorrow. She hoped she'd be able to help Mercedes think it all through.

She patted her pocket, where the twin plum pits waited. Her idea was for her and Merce to plant them on the very same day, at the precise same hour, Mercedes in her backyard in Cincinnati and Mo . . . wherever. She'd visit Merce's tree, and Merce would visit hers. The trees would grow up together, the exact same age, with the very same parent.

Tomorrow she'd tell Merce all this. Tomorrow, she had the feeling, a lot of things would be happening. But for now, the Green Kingdom stretched in front of her, rustling with its quiet secrets. For now, Mo was all alone.

"Surprise!" Dottie leaped up from behind the guardrail.

It was no use claiming she hated surprises. Besides,

did she? Mo knew she'd have to think that over later, along with so many other things. And besides again— even though she hated to admit it, Mo wasn't sorry to see her little sister. "May I ask what you think you're doing here?"

Dottie threw her hands over her head, spun around, and bowed to the street. "The dance of joy!" she proclaimed.

Dottie danced till she was dizzy, then leaned into Mo. Mo plucked potato chip crumbs from her hair.

"Mo? I really do remember stuff."

Mo's arms made a circle around her sister. All up and down Fox Street, fireflies drifted up from the grass. Mo saw Taur Baggott nab one. She steeled herself, certain he'd squish it, or stomp it, or pluck off its wings.

"We're always going to be sisters, right?"

"Right."

"Till deaf do us part."

Up on Paradise, a siren wailed, then abruptly stopped, as if it had changed its mind.

Down in the Green Kingdom, the trees rustled, holding their own thoughts secret. Hidden among them, a fox watched the night fall.

And in between stood Mo Wren, in between not just

the two poles of her beloved dead-end street, but in between so many things her head spun, as if she herself had just performed the dance of joy. Mo was tempted to shut her eyes tight, so she wouldn't have to see what she was going to have to give up, one day soon. Instead she looked. She looked at it all, people and houses and darkly shining street—she looked at it hard.

And then, wonder of wonders, as if he'd fallen under the spell of the day's many goodnesses, she saw Taur Baggott stretch his fist toward the sky. He uncurled his fingers and let that tiny bit of life go. The firefly's light meandered skyward, blinking but determined, and Mo pointed to make sure Dottie saw, too.